"I'm making it hard f[...] asked. "Asking you to [...] promise. To do something you don't want to do."

"You have a right to ask me to plea-bargain, Arianna. I'm a lawyer. That's what I do."

A smear of emotion stained her cheeks.

"Forget it, Ari," he said, more softly. "What I want doesn't matter. What you want does. I'm your lawyer. That's the relationship we have."

They both knew that what he'd just said wasn't true.

She lifted her chin a fraction of an inch and confronted him. "Maybe I care what you want."

He didn't let himself move.

"Maybe I care what you want not just as a lawyer, but as a person. As a man."

WHAT ARE *LOVESWEPT* ROMANCES?

They are stories of true romance and touching emotion. We believe those two very important ingredients are constants in our highly sensual and very believable stories in the LOVESWEPT line. Our goal is to give you, the reader, stories of consistently high quality that may sometimes make you laugh, sometimes make you cry, but are always fresh and creative and contain many delightful surprises within their pages.

Most romance fans read an enormous number of books. Those they truly love, they keep. Others may be traded with friends and soon forgotten. We hope that each LOVE-SWEPT romance will be a treasure—a "keeper." We will always try to publish

LOVE STORIES YOU'LL NEVER FORGET
BY AUTHORS YOU'LL ALWAYS REMEMBER

The Editors

Loveswept® 737

AFTER MIDNIGHT

LINDA WARREN

BANTAM BOOKS
NEW YORK · TORONTO · LONDON · SYDNEY · AUCKLAND

Special thanks to Beth Shuster,
attorney-at-law, for her generous help and advice

AFTER MIDNIGHT
A Bantam Book / April 1995

LOVESWEPT *and the wave design are registered trademarks of*
Bantam Books, a division of Bantam Doubleday Dell Publishing Group,
Inc. Registered in U.S. Patent and Trademark Office and elsewhere.

All rights reserved.
Copyright © 1995 by Linda Warren.
Back cover art copyright © 1995 by Hal Frenck.
Floral border by Lori Nelson Field.
No part of this book may be reproduced or transmitted in any
form or by any means, electronic or mechanical,
including photocopying, recording, or by any
information storage and retrieval system, without
permission in writing from the publisher.
For information address: Bantam Books.

If you would be interested in receiving protective vinyl covers for your
Loveswept books, please write to this address for information:

> *Loveswept*
> *Bantam Books*
> *P.O. Box 985*
> *Hicksville, NY 11802*

ISBN 0-553-44404-2

Published simultaneously in the United States and Canada

Bantam Books are published by Bantam Books, a division of Bantam Dou-
bleday Dell Publishing Group, Inc. Its trademark, consisting of the words
"Bantam Books" and the portrayal of a rooster, is Registered in U.S.
Patent and Trademark Office and in other countries. Marca Registrada.
Bantam Books, 1540 Broadway, New York, New York 10036.

PRINTED IN THE UNITED STATES OF AMERICA
OPM   0 9 8 7 6 5 4 3 2 1

ONE

Twenty to one she was guilty.

And Cord Prescott was going to get her off. Staring at the metal door of the holding cell, Cord sensed it, with cool, cynical certainty.

"One of these days the cops are gonna win one for a change, you know that, Prescott?" Lieutenant Garza shoved open the heavy door. "Maybe this Rossini woman's gonna be it. A crumb for the cause of justice."

"Maybe," Cord said neutrally. He didn't need to contest the point, not with Garza. The longtime cop met Cord's level gaze with acknowledgment of what they both knew: Guilty or not, she'd probably walk.

Cord was good at his job.

Garza yanked at the door. It clanged shut like the closing argument to an irrefutable case.

As if unable to leave it at that, Garza shot another comment through the bars of the viewing window. "She did it for her old man—you know that, don't you? Needed the money for his medical bills."

Cord didn't answer. He knew what prompted the comment—a cop's frustration with a system of justice that allowed lawyers like Cord to tip the scales so far off kilter that the guilty fell out. Garza's speculation was probably pretty close to the bone.

It also wasn't open to discussion. When Cord had agreed to take on Arianna Rossini's case, the question of her motives had ceased to be a possible topic of conversation. Why she'd done it was irrelevant. Or if.

He said instead, "How're your girls, Phil?"

Garza shook his head, huffed once, and reluctantly grinned. "Givin' me gray hair. The second one's decided she wants to be a cop."

"Could be worse," Cord told him. "She could've decided she wanted to be a lawyer."

"Please," Garza muttered. He shoved down the locking handle on the door.

Cord listened to the bolt lock before he turned around to face his latest client.

The woman sitting on the cot was so still, he thought for a moment she might be in shock. Her head was bent, her hair falling in front of her face in a disheveled reddish-gold tangle that looked like she'd run her fingers through it too many times. She showed no reaction at all to Cord's entrance.

He glanced over his shoulder, half considering asking Garza to call a doctor, but when he looked back at her she'd raised her head. The expression in her eyes showed a clear and lucid intelligence that stopped his half-formed request to Garza before it was spoken.

Dark, candid eyes framed by pale brows and eyelashes met his steadily, without the smallest sign of evasion. Her lips moved, as if she would speak, then thinned into a taut line of anxiety that emphasized the vulnerability of her mouth.

As if to counter that, she lifted her chin. The gesture was so slight, he might have missed it, but it was weighted with pride, determination, and a passion of purpose that could have been taken from a face in a fourteenth century Italian fresco.

A reaction reverberated through him and rearranged every preconception he'd walked in with.

Maybe she was innocent.

The thought came at him out of left field and caught him as unprepared as if he were a rookie in a preseason game. It was so irrational, he came close to letting out a bemused, I'll-be-damned laugh. What stopped him wasn't the well-oiled machinery of professionalism or even the knowledge that Garza was still within earshot.

What stopped him was the profoundly illogical sense that his reaction was true.

"Ms. Rossini?"

She nodded, once. The movement barely disturbed the fall of hair that brushed her shoulders.

"I'm Cordwell Prescott."

She didn't even blink. The dark eyes, made striking by the contrast of blond eyelashes and eyebrows, continued to study him without flinching, with none of the defensive nervousness he'd come to expect of his clients at first meetings.

Cord went on, "You spoke to my law partner, Charlie Kent, before you were brought in and booked. He talked to me, and I've agreed to represent you."

Her gaze stayed on his face. "Thank you," she said finally. Her voice was low, with a slight hesitation before she spoke, as if, having met him, she was considering him, making a judgment.

On a level that had nothing to do with business, Cord felt a stirring response, an intense interest in what that judgment was.

Irritated at himself, he took a step toward the battered table in the middle of the cell, swinging his briefcase up onto the scarred wooden surface.

He wasn't sure, at first, that she'd move from the cot, but when he snapped open the catch of the briefcase, she stood up. "If you need a retainer, I'll make the arrangements for it as soon as—"

"No. This is pro bono."

"Pro bono?" she repeated. "Does that mean you're working for nothing?"

"I'm working at Charlie's request, because I owe him the favor. If you have any objections to the pro bono rate, take them up with him."

She walked toward the other side of the table. She was tall—five seven or five eight to his six-two —slightly built, dressed in jeans, denim shirt, and a long cardigan sweater. She must not have had the chance to change from her work clothes, he realized. Or chose not to. In some contradictory way the work clothes suited her, the way a man's shirt emphasized femininity in some women.

They made her look like she didn't belong there.

He pulled a yellow legal pad from the briefcase and dropped it on the table with a decisive slap. What the hell difference did it make what she looked like, except for possible speculation on what effect her looks would have on a jury? Cord Prescott was neither young nor green, and seven years of criminal law had taken care of his excess idealism. Arianna Rossini might not look like his typical client, but there was no doubt a crime had been committed. She was the one with motive, means, and opportunity.

And then there was the evidence.

The police had that, filed away in an envelope in the evidence room where it was making District Attorney Frank Oslund smile.

Cord set his jaw, reaching into his briefcase for his pen. "I need to establish the basic facts, Ms. Rossini, before I can arrange for your bail."

"Yes. All right."

"You're a contractor, working on the renovations for one of the investment properties owned by Kent and Prescott, is that right?"

"Yes."

"My partner, Charlie Kent, hired you to do the job. You have a long-standing family friendship with him, is that true?"

She nodded. "My father does. They were friends when they were in high school." The ghost of a smile flickered over her mouth. "They played together on the soccer team."

"How long have you been running your contracting business, Ms. Rossini?"

"Seven and a half years."

"By yourself?"

"Yes."

"You're not married?"

This time her hesitation was long enough to be a statement in itself. Cord waited her out, but he silently cursed himself for asking a question that he knew was motivated more by personal curiosity than professional interests.

"I took over my father's business," she said finally. "Didn't Charlie tell you this, Mr. Prescott?" Her gaze lingered for a moment on his blank legal pad.

Cord looked down at it himself, hearing her underlying question as clearly as if she'd spoken it: *Why didn't he write this down?*

The same question, asked years ago in his father's dry, faintly contemptuous voice, echoed back through stray memories. He'd met the question then with a cocky answer: He didn't need to write down what he'd remember without notes.

His father had waited a moment, sharpening the barb, then given him one of the tenets of the profession. You don't write it for you, he'd said. You write it for the law. For the jury. For the client. You write it so they'll know you can't be had.

Cord hadn't had an answer to that one. Not then, not in words. His answer had been to become as tough as the old man had been. Tougher, even more cynical. Less easily had.

He squeezed his fingers around the pen, tapped it on the pad. Then, in a gesture unexpected enough to make her flinch, he tossed the pen down on the dingy wooden table and straightened to his full height, propping his hands on his hips.

"The case against you is pretty damning, Ms. Rossini. If you're found guilty, you could do a lot of years in prison. I want to make sure we both understand the facts."

Even in the dim light he could see the color drain from her face, see her swallow hard, and Cord Prescott felt another emotion that didn't belong there: Apology. Regret for the harsh reminder she hadn't needed.

He was the one who'd needed it.

"The facts are," she said finally, her voice a

little too controlled, a little too calm, "that I've been contracted by Charlie to do renovations on the town house next door to your firm's office, where Charlie plans to move his office space and leave the old offices to you. The building has historic significance. There was a grant application, to the Massachusetts Inner City Heritage Preservation Fund, for money to help cover the renovation costs. The grant was approved and the state's been sending out the money, but it seems to be . . ." She faltered for the first time, glancing down at her hands.

"Missing?" he prompted.

She swallowed, then raised her gaze to his face, the steady, dark eyes strikingly eloquent. "Someone's been submitting false invoices for work not done. The auditing firm for the preservation fund called me this morning and told me they wanted to examine my records. They found some of the false invoices in my desk. The police were waiting outside. They came in and . . . arrested me."

"They had a warrant?"

She nodded. "The auditors had notified them earlier. The warrant had already been issued when they called me."

Which meant they'd been pretty sure of themselves, Cord reflected. But he'd known that before he walked into the cell. "The checks from the state have been coming to a P.O. box rented in the name of the building's owners—Charlie and his out-of-state investment partners—is that right?"

"Yes. Someone's been . . . forging my signature to cash them."

Cord reached for the pen and picked it up again, though he made no notation on the pad. "Someone who knew the progress of the job and had access to the books. Who does that include?"

There was a short silence. This was the time when clients made profuse protestations of innocence, and anyone-could-have-done-it accusations.

She didn't give him the typical answer. She waited a moment, considering the question, then said, her voice even, "I can't imagine any of my crew doing this. They've worked for me for years. I don't see how the owners could have seen my books. I can't think of anyone else." She took a deep breath, then let it out. "Except me, of course."

For reasons he couldn't begin to analyze, Cord felt his complex, contradictory reaction to her stretch to accommodate an admiration he'd seldom felt for a client. Never, he thought, for a woman who stirred him the way this one did.

She wasn't what he'd expected; he knew that much. What unbalanced him was the idea that after too many years in this business, he could still be shocked by something that didn't meet his expectations. His habit of objectivity was so ingrained, he thought of it as part of his nature, yet he caught himself calculating the number of years it had been since he'd let himself wonder if a client was innocent.

"Does that represent the facts as we both understand them, Mr. Prescott?"

He let the silence draw out between them, while distant footsteps slapped against the floor outside and their sense of isolation increased.

She hadn't said a word to the police, Cord knew. Maybe the strain of holding it in would make her spill it now. He was too good a lawyer not to recognize the opportunity. He'd been too tough for too long to let it go by, despite the illogical emotions that had taken him by surprise. He knew what the situation called for now. Some finely gauged pressure, a careful, surgical probe for the key information—and he'd have what he needed, whether or not the client had intended to give it up.

She crossed her arms in front of her, hugging the elbows of her long sweater. In a gesture that contradicted the set of her chin, the straightness of her shoulders, she lifted one hand to her throat and closed her fingers around a pendant he hadn't seen because she wore it inside the collar of her shirt.

Her hand was shaking. A faint red mark encircled her wrist, left by the handcuffs.

Cord felt something tighten in his gut. Something that cut through his attorney's expertise like fire through ice. Two heartbeats later he knew what it was: The desire to touch her. The urge washed over him, an unexplainable impulse that defied words and transcended the dingy, institutional walls of the police holding cell. He wanted to touch her. Brush back the tangled hair. Make her smile. Give himself a reason to justify the not-quite-conscious fantasy that had, for reasons he couldn't analyze, taken root in his jaded imagination like some unlikely wildflower in his lawn-serviced backyard.

He sucked in a harsh breath of reality, letting the surroundings hit him with all the depressing, cynical overtones accumulated year by year in the holding cell of the Worcester, Massachusetts Superior Court.

This wasn't about planning a defense, he told himself. This was about Cord Prescott wanting to hear Arianna Rossini tell him she was innocent.

And it wasn't going to happen. He wouldn't let himself ask her, wouldn't let himself believe her if she said the words.

He dragged the folding chair out from the table and sat down in it, mentally dragging back his lapsed focus. "Let's start with the preliminaries. How did those invoices get into your desk?"

"I have no idea."

No idea. And no help. He made himself discount the possibility that it was true.

"Any guesses? Speculation? Possibilities?"

Silence. When he glanced up at her, she'd

gone still, her eyes steady on his face, both hands gripped around her elbows again.

"I don't plan to contest the charge," she said clearly. "So you don't need to plan a defense."

A protest slammed against the surface of his practiced, professional neutrality. *No contest.* It was tantamount to a guilty plea.

Disillusionment shored up the cynicism that had become so habitual, he'd only noticed its absence.

He set his jaw and kept his voice level. "You understand the implications of nolo contendere?" he asked her. "No possibility for defense? Mitigating circumstances considered only at the discretion of the court?"

"Yes."

"You'd essentially be admitting guilt, Ms. Rossini. Do you understand that?"

He couldn't read her face. Her reaction was evident only in some indefinable sense of loss that passed through the small, close room like darkening light. He wasn't sure if it came from her, or from him.

She pulled her sweater more tightly around her, hunching her shoulders as if she were cold, though the temperature in the holding cell was, as usual, warmer than was comfortable for Cord. "Can you keep me out of jail with a no contest plea?" she asked finally.

He studied her a moment, then picked up his

belongings, snapped the briefcase shut, and stood. "Probably. But you'd end up with a stiff fine, a lengthy period of probation, possible loss of your contractor's license, your business, your professional reputation."

She let out a long breath. "The case against me is pretty damning, as you said."

"That doesn't mean it's in your best interest to plead guilty."

"I'm not pleading guilty. I want to plead no contest. There's a difference."

"There's no substantive difference in the eyes of the law, Ms. Rossini. And as your attorney, I don't recommend this course of action."

Her mouth curved, just slightly, in an expression that could be called a smile only if he couldn't see her eyes. "But you have to follow my instructions, don't you?"

"Yes," he said, too curtly.

Her smile faded. "I'm sorry," she said. Her voice was low, and had a husky note in it that shot through Cord with palpable force. "I didn't mean that arrogantly or sarcastically. I'm—grateful for your help."

Cord's antagonism washed out of him like a receding tide, leaving a pool of emotional magnetism that muddied every professional tenet he took for granted. What the hell was Arianna Rossini about? And what the hell had she done to knock him so far off course, he was struggling to deal with something as irrelevant as gratitude from a client?

"You don't have to worry about my feelings, Ms. Rossini," he said. "Under the circumstances, you're entitled to worry more about your own."

"But I—" She broke off, then she smiled again, just slightly. She shook her head, working her hands into the pockets of her sweater and turning away from him. "Never mind. The law isn't about feelings anyway."

"It's not supposed to be."

She glanced back at him, frowning at the tone of his voice. Her dark eyes were wary, evaluative, seeing too much. "No," she said. "It's supposed to be about justice. But it isn't always, is it?"

No, it wasn't always, he thought. Not when a good defense lawyer found a useful technicality, or a fine point on which to hang a jury. Not when the accused was defended by Kent & Prescott. Cord kept his face impassive, but he had an uncanny feeling she could read his thoughts.

"Charlie says you're the best defense lawyer in the city," she said into the silence. "You're well known for getting acquittals out of cases no one else would try, he said."

"Did he? Well, I won't hesitate to use him for a reference again," Cord said ironically.

"Has he taken cases for you too? Is that why you owe him?"

He paused for a moment, considering his answer to the frank question, then said, "I owe him because when I was a kid working in the law office, and my father spent a good deal of his time pointing out my mistakes, Charlie always came through with a root beer and a vote of confidence."

"I guess you've proved him right, then. He talked as though getting me acquitted would be a sure thing."

Cord wondered if she'd heard what she wanted to hear in that phone call instead of what his partner had said. Charlie was rarely so impetuous as to promise an acquittal. "Not a sure thing," he said slowly.

"I can't afford to go to jail, Mr. Prescott. I'm needed. My father can't get along without me. He depends on me. There isn't anyone else he'd allow . . . to take care of him. He needs me." The words were carefully modulated, controlled, but the urgency behind them came through as clearly as if she'd shouted. Her shoulders were tense with it, her straight back rigid. "I love him," she said. "I can't afford to risk that on the law's *justice*."

Cord stared at her, one part of his brain automatically processing the information—mitigating circumstances, her father's dependence—while another part put its own meaning on what she'd said and reacted to it with a flicker of feeling that was far too close to emotional involvement.

She glanced around the cell, then looked at him again. There was a sheen of moisture in her eyes, the first sign of tears she'd shown. "I can't go to jail, Mr. Prescott."

"Did the police mistreat you in any way?"

She shook her head.

Cord let out a breath.

"I'm going to get you out of here," he said abruptly as tension stretched across the air of the cell like a tightening web. "I should be able to arrange bail right away, if I drop a hint to the police that you're not planning to contest. The conditions will be that you cease and desist any work at the job site under investigation, and you and your crew are restrained from any visits to the premises. That's acceptable to you?"

She nodded as he stood up and lifted his briefcase from the table. "You'll be all right until then?"

She nodded again, then, after a moment's hesitation, held out her hand to him.

Her skin was cool against his palm, smooth except for the ridge of calluses along the base of her fingers. Her small, boyish hand trembled, though she tried to hide it under a strong carpenter's grip.

In Cord's mind an image flickered. A willow grew in a tiny park between the police barracks and the courthouse, planted there years ago by a landscape gardener who had more faith in the soil than experience. The tree, against all odds, flourished, graceful, self-contained, green amidst the gray stone buildings. Living proof of vibrant, elemental, irrational forces that couldn't be controlled by logic and weren't dictated by probable cause.

With ruthless self-discipline Cord wiped out the complex, inappropriate emotions that lay just under the surface of that image.

It couldn't happen.

Nothing could happen between them.

He dropped her hand, then pushed the metal chair back under the table, took a step toward the door, and slapped its heavy metal surface twice. The sound echoed along the empty corridor outside the cell.

He had a moment to wait for Garza to come and let him out. It was a moment too long. Cord turned back toward her. She was watching him, her face alive with the subtle nuances of emotion he'd taken at first for composure, one hand touching the necklace again—a delicate ivory cameo on a gold chain.

A question burned in his brain. He didn't ask it, but her eyes widened and a tint of color, visible even in the sickly light, washed into her face.

Something unspoken stretched between them, humming with possible futures, all of them precipitous, unmapped, unwise. All of them dangerous.

She drew herself up, lifted her chin, and met his narrowed gaze. "No, I didn't do it."

Garza's steps scraped down the hallway, then

the bolt banged against the stop and the door swung open.

Cord walked out of the cell and followed the policeman down the hallway, wondering with every step what the hell had just happened to him.

TWO

"You're free, lady."

The policeman who'd just yanked back the door scowled at her as if he hadn't wanted to open it.

Arianna got to her feet, struggling against confusion. "But I thought . . . don't you have questions?"

The officer shrugged. "Apparently not. Your lawyer arranged it."

"My lawyer . . ." Her thoughts were scattered, her composure stretched to the limit, but the image of Cord Prescott coalesced in her mind, reassuring and disturbing at the same time. He'd arranged it, the policeman had said. She was free to go. She ushered up a swift prayer of thanks and walked out of the cell.

She could get through this, she told herself. She just had to keep in mind that cool, detached attorney's image, the expertise that had arranged her release, the sense that this was all just a series of legal maneuvers that had nothing to do with real people or real feelings.

Or a handclasp that had stirred emotions too dangerous to think about now.

"Arianna!"

From across the station room Pop called her name and hurried across the floor toward her, clutching his hat in his hands, his face ashen.

She made a choked sound of protest. "Pop. What are you doing here? Who called you?" She shot a glance toward Cord Prescott, standing beside the main desk. Had he called her father? Could he do that without asking her?

"Arianna, what is this?" Pop said, ignoring her questions.

There was no way to protect him now, she thought with dismay. He'd have to have the whole truth—if he didn't have it already. "I've been arrested, Pop."

"Arrested! For what?"

She told him, as briefly as possible, watching his face grow darker with every grim fact: The forged checks, the false invoices for construction work not actually done, the evidence found in her desk.

She could see the rage building in his eyes before she'd finished speaking. "They think *you* . . . ?"

"Yes, Pop. They think I'm the most . . . likely one."

"They think *you* did this? They think it was *you?*"

Pop's rising voice drew a few glances from the officers in the station room, and Cord Prescott was watching the exchange levelly, making her conscious of Pop's words and the effect they might have.

"Pop," she said, trying to calm him, "it will be all right. I've worked out a plan, with my lawyer. It will be all right."

"How could they think *you* did this? How could they be stupid enough to think *you* did this?"

Into the too-attentive silence from the station room, Cord Prescott stepped forward and put his hand casually on Arianna's elbow. "Mr. Rossini," he said smoothly, "I don't know who called you. But the important fact now is that your daughter is free to go. I think that's what she needs. Would you take her home?"

The appeal to his paternal instincts quieted Pop's agitation as no reprimand could have. He took Ari's elbow from Cord and drew her protectively closer, frowning at the lawyer but not, at least, berating the police.

"You're the lawyer?"

"I'm the lawyer," Cord said.

Pop let out his breath. "Come on, *cara*," he murmured to Ari.

Cord handed her the envelope of her belongings and a form to sign. She scribbled her name, nodded her thanks, and let Pop walk her out to the car.

"Should I drive, Pop?" she asked, as always.

"You don't have to."

"It's all right. I'd like to."

He conceded, with old-world chivalry, to her wishes. She took the keys from him and let him hand her into the car, then waited while he got into the passenger side.

She gripped the steering wheel hard to steady the trembling of her hands, then slid the key into the ignition. It rattled slightly against the lock.

"How could this happen, Arianna?" he asked brokenly.

She didn't answer him. She didn't need to. He knew. He knew it too well, exactly how it could happen. She glanced toward him and saw the same incredulous outrage in his eyes that she felt herself.

They were both silent on the short drive home.

The house was a shingled Victorian on one of Worcester's old tree-lined streets. The ornate wooden structure provided Pop with ample scope for his perpetual renovation projects. Ari pulled into the driveway and parked beside a stack of new lumber.

Her gaze traveled over the porch. "You sanded some of the railing," she commented.

"Yah."

"You're going to refinish it?"

"It needs refinishing."

She glanced toward him. He must have worked all afternoon. Longer than he should have. And then to have this shock . . .

He was scowling at her, grim, wearing that expression he used to cover up his worry. "Maybe I could make us some coffee, Pop? I could use a cup of coffee."

"Mm," her father said, nodding. "I'll make it."

Ari let him walk in ahead of her, knowing he needed something to occupy his hands, to calm himself.

She followed more slowly, stopping at the porch landing, her hand on the carved post beside the stairs. This piece of railing Pop wouldn't refinish. It had been put up, with his help, by her nieces, Gina and Gabie. There were dents in the smooth, curved wood, where her nieces had missed with their hammers. Pop would leave that railing in place forever. He treasured those marks.

She touched one of the indentions, imagining Gina and Gabie as grown women who'd be teased, someday, by their grandfather about their youthful inexperience. It was a good thought. One she wanted to hold on to, as an antidote to the bad ones.

There'd been times, just after Pop got back from prison, when she'd found hammer marks that hadn't been made by childish mistakes.

They'd been intentional—angry, bitter protests of a cruel twist of fate. Those she'd repaired as soon as Pop had healed enough to let her. Some she'd replaced twice. The bad days had diminished slowly for him, erratically.

She closed her hand around the banister, pressing her palm against the lathed wood, feeling the straightness of the grain and the smoothness of the finish. Then she let it go and went through the front door into the hallway.

The kitchen was filled with the smell of coffee from the automatic espresso machine. Pop had gotten out two cups with spoons. On the table was a five-pound bag of sugar and a carton of cream.

When she looked at him again, he'd picked up one of the cups, gripping it so tightly, she was afraid the china would break.

"Listen to me, Arianna," he said. "Listen to me. I won't have it. You won't go to jail. I won't have that. I won't let that happen."

"Pop—"

"No! I'll go. They can take me!"

"No, Pop."

He banged the cup down on the counter, making her jump.

"No, Pop," she said again. "No one's going to jail."

He stared at her, his chin jutted out, his square jaw set and stubborn.

"You know that?" he demanded. "You can say that?"

"Yes, I can. I have a lawyer. I told you that."
She made herself take a breath and let it out
slowly, while the picture of the holding cell's
dingy walls and smell of desperation washed over
her. Along with those memories was, again, the
image of the man who had walked into that cell
and thoroughly, violently, catapulted her emotions into confusion. The man who had looked
straight into her eyes as if he could read her soul;
touched her hand and turned the confusion to
shock when she'd felt the unexpected response of
her body.

"I'm not going to fight it, Pop," she said, a
little too urgently. She had to take a breath to
bring her voice under control. "I'm going to make
a deal with the prosecutor, plead no contest. And
my lawyer says he'll keep me out of jail."

"This lawyer I met?"

"Yes."

"Charlie Kent sent him over, didn't he?"

It was the logical conclusion. She'd been
working for Charlie. "Yes, Pop."

Her father made a sound of disgust. "What
kind of lawyer tells you to make a deal like that?"

What kind of lawyer? The question jarred her
into silence, her answer caught between the
straightforward facts and her own disturbing reaction to Cord Prescott.

What kind of lawyer? Tough. Ruthless. Cynical in his manipulation of the legal system. The
kind of lawyer who wouldn't ask if the woman he

was about to represent was guilty, yet who'd taken the case because he owed a debt of root beer and kindness to his partner. The kind of man who took crime and betrayal and deceit as the staple properties of his trade, but who seemed to operate within a code of personal ethics she couldn't have imagined before she'd been accused of a crime she didn't commit, then handcuffed, arrested, locked in a cell. Cord Prescott was the kind of man she should have no business with.

But she did. He was a man for a desperate woman.

"A lawyer who's very good at his job, Pop."

"Lawyers are lawyers," he said stubbornly.

"No," she said more slowly. "Not this one."

Disbelief flared in her father's eyes. "You think I'll like this one?"

The image of Cord Prescott flickered in her mind again, the aura of power he wore like an expensive suit, as if it belonged to him. The wide, mobile stretch of his mouth that could express emotions so elegantly, and so subtly; that could form the cogent, precise expressions of the law with arrogant ease. The eyes, intelligent and curious, their gray color almost brilliant in its intense focus. Too observant, too knowing. Devoid of innocence.

"No. You won't like him, Pop."

Her father shook his head, looking away.

"When he came into the . . . station." She didn't say *jail*. It was a word she would never say around her father. "The policeman there said, 'Why don't you let the cops win one for a change?' You could tell they already thought they wouldn't win this case. Not against him. He'll get this deal if he says he will. He gets whatever he wants. I think he doesn't stop until he gets it."

Her father was frowning at her.

"He's Charlie's partner, Pop," she said. "Cord Prescott."

"Charlie's partner?" Pop's voice shook with surprise. "Prescott's son?"

"Yes."

"He works with Charlie?"

"Charlie's a good lawyer, Pop," she said quietly. "If you'd taken his advice you wouldn't have—"

She broke off, unwilling to bring up the subject they never discussed.

"And this is what Prescott wants you to do? This *no contest*? Letting them think you did it?"

"It's what I decided myself, before I even met him. It's what I told him I wanted."

Her father's mouth twisted. He shook his head, staring down at the counter beside the coffee maker, then flattened his hand on the butcherblock wood, spreading his fingers in a gesture she recognized. Drawing strength from the wood, comfort from the texture of the grain. "You're not like me," he said softly. "Not stubborn. Not pigheaded."

"Pop." It should be easier, caring about people, she thought, feeling the weight of that burden across her shoulders. It should be easier to know what they needed, and what she could give. What she could afford to give. She stepped close to him and put her hand on his arm.

He nodded and covered her hand with his own, and she leaned her forehead against his shoulder. "I'm enough like you, Pop," she murmured. "I've tried to be anyway. In all the important ways."

His arm came around her shoulders and squeezed, pulling her close to him. She could feel him trembling. "This lawyer, this Cord Prescott. He knows you didn't do it?"

Did he? The question rippled through her, leaving a trail of urgency that was out of proportion to its place in her emotions.

"It doesn't matter, Pop. He doesn't need to know that to do his job."

It doesn't matter. The words echoed false in her heart. She knew it mattered. Faith, trust, belief in the truth—that was the concrete foundation of her life.

Pop pushed her a little bit away from him, holding her by the shoulders, staring into her face. "But you told him?"

"Yes."

"And he didn't believe you."

"I don't think he can believe anyone," she said slowly.

"Then you're right," Pop said, his voice hardening. "I don't like him."

With no other warning, regret gripped her, tight in her chest. She'd given Cord Prescott the truth, though he hadn't asked for it, hadn't wanted it, maybe. She'd given it because she'd needed to, because for some reason she couldn't fathom in this frightening tangle of events, she'd had to give a man she'd never met before some small basis for having faith.

She didn't know why. She didn't know anything about the strange emotions she felt at the thought of Cord Prescott, except that they were ambivalent, chaotic, and dangerous.

"I don't know if I like him either, Pop," she whispered, into his shoulder. "But it doesn't matter. I need him."

"So she told you she didn't do it."

Charlie Kent leaned back in one of Cord's office chairs and jerked at his formal club tie, loosening it. The knot ending up slightly askew.

"That's right," Cord said.

"No explanation of where the invoices came from? No mention of anyone she might have been working with?"

Cord's desk was littered with law briefs and computer printouts, none of which had shed a candlepower's worth of light on Arianna Rossini's case. He pushed himself away from the desk and paced across the office to a window, leaning one shoulder against the casing that framed a fifth-floor view of the city's renovated downtown area, now softened by evening light. "No," he said. "No mention of anyone."

"Come on," Charlie muttered. "I've known her all her life. I never pegged her for this, but give me a break. They must've gotten there some-how. Poltergeists? Gremlins? The tax auditor was a jealous ex-boyfriend?"

Cord turned back to his partner but didn't an-swer. Charlie propped an Italian leather loafer on his opposite knee and tapped his toe against the edge of Cord's desk, treating trousers and pol-ished wood with the same carelessness he'd used for as long as Cord could remember. As a boy visiting this office Cord had been amazed when his father's partner would put his feet up on the desk and use his loosened tie to wipe out a crystal glass before offering Cord a root beer.

"What?" Charlie said. He raised his hands and shrugged with the mock innocence of a mafioso confronted by a streetwise cop. "She oughta get out of jail free because she said she didn't do it and her admittedly well-placed assets are one hell of a distraction?"

Cord shoved himself away from the window, clamping his jaw shut. That same overly cynical question had plagued him since he walked into the holding cell, but he didn't have any answer he could speak aloud to Charlie. A glib, clever comment about sex, maybe. That he could say. But it wasn't sex that had unhinged his trial-schooled logic. It was something else.

He could feel that response now, the same way he'd felt it when she'd stood in front of him, her shoulders straight, but with her fists buried in the elbows of her sweater and marks from the handcuffs circling her wrists.

"She doesn't want to get out of jail free," he said, making his voice stay even. "She wants to plead nolo."

"*Nolo?*" Charlie gave a huff of amusement. "What the hell has she been doing—reading medieval law books?"

"I thought maybe she'd been reading helpful hints from the D.A.'s office."

"Yeah." Charlie grinned. "D.A. Oslund would be happy if she made his job that easy, wouldn't he?" He ran a palm over thinning blond hair, then laced his fingers over his comfortable paunch. "Well, it seems to me you got three choices, kid. You can plead innocent and take it to trial. You can plead guilty and take your knocks. Or you can play the game and cut her some kind of a deal that'll keep her out of jail."

Some kind of a deal. Where she'd admit her guilt and Cord would plea-bargain it down to minimal terms of payment. His jaw clenched again in a protest he wouldn't let himself show. "What's her old man got to do with this?" he asked.

Charlie straightened in the chair, pulled a face, then met Cord's narrowed gaze. "Something I suppose I should have told you before you agreed to take the case," he admitted ruefully. "He went to prison ten, eleven years ago. Did three years of an eight-year sentence."

". . . And?"

"The crime was embezzlement. I represented him. Lost the case."

Cord swore into the explosive silence, low, succinct, and graphic enough to elicit a reaction from the usually unflappable Charlie.

"He was a hell of a client, dammit. Insisted on takin' the case to trial. Stonewalled on the stand, like the jury wouldn't dare find him guilty. He had a massive heart attack when he was in," Charlie went on. "He was paroled out after that. She supports him. She's still paying off his medical bills."

"She's got financial problems?"

A muscle quirked in Charlie's face. Neither man had to spell out that they were talking about motive in a crime, not family finances. "I don't know how bad her money problems are," Charlie said finally. "I made it a point to see she got this renovation job for us. I put in a word for her for half the other jobs she's done too. She wouldn't take money. Not," he added, giving the words a pause, "from me, anyway."

"That doesn't mean she took it from the Commonwealth of Massachusetts, dammit!"

Staring at his partner, Charlie lifted his hands,

palms out, in a gesture of disarmed intention. "I didn't say she did."

Cord let out a long breath and ran a hand through his hair. "I'm sorry. That wasn't aimed at you."

Silence stretched out between them, taut and awkward for a moment, then Charlie levered himself up from the chair. He walked across the mellow-toned carpet to the cabinet built into the shelves that held Cord's law library. Some of the volumes had been given to him by his father.

The silver decanter of brandy was brought out on ritual occasions, as it had been when Cord's father occupied this office, and the same crystal snifters were kept behind it in the cabinet. Charlie got out two of them, brought them back to the desk, and poured out a measure of the dark, aromatic liquor.

Cord watched, taking in the gesture, recognizing it for what it was: A reminder of what Cord had earned in the past few years since his father's death—prestige, respect, a reputation that would have made his father acknowledge him as an equal.

That had been more than enough compensation for his loss of idealism, Cord told himself, taking the offered glass. So why the hell was he arguing with his partner?

He was too old for naïveté.

He was too old to start dropping his protective cynicism.

And he was way too old to let a woman make him feel as if she were the doorway to that lost idealism.

The wood was cherry, fine-grained, aromatic, cool under her hands as Ari slid the piece of wainscoting into place and tapped in a finish nail. The precise, rhythmic sound of the small hammer resonated through the empty room. Her crew had left for the day, but she had stayed to begin the artisan's work of fitting the cabinetry, and to let the familiar, skilled motions of her hands act as a balm to her spirit.

It was a healing thing, to have work that she loved. Something she could thank Pop for, she reflected, sitting back on her heels and examining the fit of the wood. It was one of the ways she was like him, though he was right to think there were ways she wasn't like him.

Not wanting to fight this case in court, for instance. Letting Cord Prescott make a deal for her.

What kind of lawyer? Pop had asked again, late last night.

Not, what's his plan, or what does he think will happen? but, what kind of lawyer?

The question had haunted her. Or maybe her answer. *He has his own idea of what's right, Pop. And I think he always does it.*

Pop had ended the conversation with finality

after that answer. He'd changed the subject and brushed off her question of who had called him when she was arrested. He'd made tiramisù, sweet and rich with brandy and espresso and the mascarpone cheese he wasn't supposed to have, and they'd shared it.

Ari's thoughts had been on Cord Prescott, though, a man she'd never met before who was suddenly bound up in the most wrenchingly intimate parts of her life. He'd been with her, one way or another, since she'd met him. In her thoughts, her distractions, the way she worked.

She turned to pick up another panel, and he was standing in the doorway across the room, one hand in his pants' pocket, his tie off and his shirt unbuttoned at the collar, his presence startling enough to make her pulse skip. She felt for a moment as if she'd conjured him.

She set the wood down against the wall, wiped her palms on the seat of her chinos, and turned the rest of the way to face him, ignoring her racing pulse. The dark hair, which the day before had been brushed perfectly into place, was unruly, and his suit jacket was open over the hard musculature of his shoulders and chest. His posture was relaxed, one shoulder propped against the doorframe, but in the slanting late-afternoon light his eyes were a more intense shade of gray than she had let herself remember. The lines in his face spoke too clearly of the depth of experience she'd sensed when he'd walked into her jail cell.

Neither of them spoke, but she was aware of the words that stretched across the space between them: The question he hadn't asked, the answer she'd given him without the asking. Something else rose between them too: A physical sensitivity that she couldn't deny, as if their corners and planes were being aligned, trued to a single plumb line.

She realized she'd been staring too long. She shrugged, shaking her head and giving him a slight, embarrassed smile. "Hello."

"I wasn't sure you were here," he said. "Your truck's not out front."

"One of my carpenters is using it to pick up supplies." To her relief, her voice sounded casual. "We got a little behind today."

"That's why you're working so late?"

He'd stuffed his tie into one pocket. He was working late too, she thought. Or did he work always on Saturdays? "I had to reassign the crew at your office renovation. And then—" She made a small gesture and smiled briefly. "I had to explain why."

He nodded. "You told them they're not to go near the site."

"Yes. I told them."

"And that will do it? You trust them to stay away?"

She stared at him a moment, taken aback at the notion that she wouldn't trust her own crew. "Yes. I told them it was the law."

He smiled, a quirk of the mouth at one corner, a little crooked. "That's not always a guarantee of obedience, Ms. Rossini."

"They know it's a condition of my bail. And I know them. I've worked with the same crew for years."

He let out a long breath, then looked away from her, examining the woodwork in the room with casual interest. When he looked back at her the expression in his eyes was speculative, curious, maybe a little guarded with thoughts she could only guess. "You know, then," he said, "that your head carpenter occasionally moonlights for another builder. And your apprentice has a record. Stealing cars. Four years ago."

A few blank seconds passed before it occurred to her that he was suggesting Victor and Andy as suspects. The notion was so alien, she couldn't bring herself to feel anything but bafflement at the implied accusations. "Yes, I know those things."

His expression didn't change, but some thought more serious and darker came into his eyes. "Someone connected with that renovation committed a crime, Ms. Rossini."

Anger wedged its way into her voice. "Andy was sixteen when he was caught stealing a car. He hasn't been in any trouble since. And my head carpenter takes extra jobs. Why shouldn't he? Some of his family are in Puerto Rico. He sends them money when he can. That's not a crime!"

"No. That's not a crime. As far as I know, neither one of them has committed a crime."

She felt her throat tighten. Unconsciously she reached for the board she'd leaned against the wainscoting. Picking it up, she held it braced against her thighs, running her hands along the edge. "Why are you here, Mr. Prescott?"

He didn't evade her question, or deflect it with social niceties. He met her eyes squarely and pushed himself off the doorframe, shoving both hands into his pockets. "I want you to plead not guilty at the arraignment."

Ari stood still, staring at him, letting the small shock of his unexpected statement pass through her. She should have anticipated it, she realized belatedly. That was why he'd been investigating her crew. It was what he'd wanted yesterday, when he'd met with her, when he'd asked her how the invoices could have gotten into her desk. She hadn't seen it coming, though. She was caught off guard, distracted by her personal reaction to a man she shouldn't be thinking of in personal terms at all.

Trying to cope with her confusion, she tightened her grip on the wood and shook her head. "No."

"Listen, Arianna." He took a step toward her, one hand raised, palm up. "I want you to listen to this. This is advice of counsel. You don't have to take it, but if you're going to refuse to hear it, there's no point in my representing you."

She took a breath, jolted out of her confusion as much by his use of her name as by his other words. "All right," she said, with her voice tight. "I'm listening."

"Good." He lowered his hand. "First ground rule of our relationship. I give you legal advice. You're not bound to take it, but if you choose to act in a way that contradicts it, I retain the right to formally state that you're acting against the advice of counsel."

"Mr. Prescott—"

"Second ground rule. You call me Cord. We're equal partners in this deal."

She made herself take it in, process the words, assess them. "All right. But I'm not sure there's any point in your representing me at all. For you, I mean. Charlie offered to do this for nothing, but I wouldn't have accepted if I thought it involved . . . a lot of work."

"Charlie's call, Arianna," he said briskly. "Pro bono."

"I can afford to pay you, Mr. Prescott."

He hesitated a moment. "I know that."

"You . . . ?"

"I did a cursory investigation of your financial status. It goes to motive."

"Motive?"

She must have looked as shocked as she felt. He let out a long breath and swiped a hand through his hair again. "A technicality. Just part of my job, okay?"

She said nothing, watching him.

"There are some other technicalities on this case too. The judge who's scheduled to preside at the bench trial if you plead no contest is known to be tough on these cases. He gives jail time. He's not inclined to listen to mitigating circumstances."

Her chest felt constricted. She swallowed hard. "I don't—"

"Listen, Arianna." He closed the distance between them and gripped her shoulders, holding her in place, insisting she confront him directly.

She saw him for one unbalancing moment the way he'd looked in the dull light of the holding cell when he'd turned back to her and she'd spoken the truth. He wasn't concerned with "technicalities" or the choosing of judges. He was telling her something deeper than that.

Stopped by surprise, she stared into his face. The heat of his hands burned through her flannel shirt, and a slew of intense emotions welled up from some place deep inside her, threatening every assumption she'd made about Cord Prescott and her relationship to him.

Why had she thought this would be simple? Why had she thought anything about this would be simple?

To her immense relief he let go of her, but he held her with his gaze as if he were still touching her. "The point of pleading not guilty is to take this case to conference and arrange a plea bargain."

She swallowed down her protest.

"Your case won't ever come to trial. We'll plead it out. But no contest isn't an option anymore."

She shut her eyes, wishing fiercely that she could shut out reality the same way. When she opened them again he was still watching her, his gaze steady, unrelenting, determined.

"Why not?" she asked.

"Because any judge on the bench who knew your father's prison record would think you're guilty. You wouldn't stand a chance of getting off without jail time."

Something in his look brought complete realization sluicing through her like cold flood water. "You didn't know," she said, disbelieving. "When you bailed me out yesterday, you didn't know about my father."

"No."

"But—"

"Charlie told me. Yesterday afternoon."

He hadn't known. Unreality pressed in on her, like a weight against her chest, taking her breath. If he had known, would he have been so ready to believe she wasn't guilty?

She clenched her jaw, making herself face how much it mattered to her that he cared whether she was innocent.

More than it should. More than she could let it.

She swallowed hard. The compulsion to say it again rose in her throat. She fought it, pushing it down with Pop's image, Pop's needs, her own beliefs.

"If no one's going to believe I'm innocent," she said finally, bitterly, "then what difference does it make if I plead not guilty at the arraignment?"

The silence was long enough to take a shape, to occupy space in the room, to argue against her passionate, protesting outrage at the injustice of this false accusation.

"Because that's the way the system works, Arianna."

She raised her eyes, trying to find her way through a swirl of rebellious anger to the logic of her scattered thoughts. It took effort to concentrate on what he'd said.

That's the way the system works.

She supposed it was. Hard, tough, cynical. Like Cord Prescott. And there was no doubt that he knew how to manipulate the system. How to argue, how to set up a deal.

"The *system* sent my father to jail," she said. Her voice shook a little.

"I don't intend for that to happen to you."

"Then what *do* you intend?"

"I intend to convince the D.A. he wouldn't win this case if it went to trial."

"Prove I'm innocent, you mean?"

Feelings vibrated in the air like wood dust, substantive, suspended.

"I can't prove that," he said. "What I can prove is that someone else could have done it. If I do my job, I can convince the prosecutors that someone else probably did."

"Who?"

He swung around, his back to her, and ran his hand through his hair again. When he turned to her once more his flint-gray eyes were assessing and emotionless. "Whoever is the most convincing suspect."

"My crew? Andy? Joe? Victor?" Disbelief lifted her voice.

Some emotion flared in his eyes, something strong enough to burn, but it was overlaid by a complex web of intellect and calculation. Legal concepts. The plan for a defense strategy. "I'll do whatever's necessary to argue your case," he said levelly.

Ari felt a chill settle down her spine as she took in the implications of his words.

Whatever's necessary. Not truth. Not reality. Not even, perhaps, adherence to strict justice.

Something hollow sank in her stomach, and disbelief shortened her breath. "You're talking about my father, aren't you? You're going to tell the D.A. my father did this."

"No. That's not my job, and it won't be necessary. I'm not going to file accusatory motions against anyone."

The legalistic phrase froze her down to her toes, then a flare of anger replaced it, pushing heat into her face and her voice. "Meaning what? You're just going to imply? Just plant suspicions?"

He was silent.

"The answer is no," she said, lifting her chin. "No, I won't agree to this. Not to the plea, not to the conference, and not to accusing my father of something he didn't do, for the second time in his life!"

"Arianna—" He gestured, palm open, but her own anger kept her from reading anything in his face.

"No! I've heard your advice, and I won't take it! I won't expect you to represent me now." She brushed past him, shoving her hand into her pocket for keys. She yanked open the front door of the house and held it, glaring back at him. "I'm going home. You'll have to leave."

His jaw clenched in frustration, but he strode past her out the door, then turned to watch her lock up.

"Your truck's not here," he said when she started down the steps. "I'll give you a ride."

"No, thanks."

She heard him mutter something as she took the steps double time, then broke into a run toward the sidewalk. She didn't turn to acknowledge him.

There was a cab halfway along the block, and she headed toward it, flagging it down on her way. To her relief, the cabbie saw her, pulled out into the street, and rolled to a stop in front of her. She reached for the door.

Cord caught up with her before she'd pulled the door open. He took her hand off the handle and guided her away from the cab with one arm around her shoulders.

"I'll give the lady a ride home, Hank," he said to the cabbie. "Sorry for the inconvenience."

"Whatever you say, Counselor."

Ari watched the cab pull away, detesting the urge she felt to break down and scream as if she were still a little girl who could be forgiven a tantrum. She'd already given up enough of her dignity in Cord Prescott's presence. It would be stupid and futile to lose the rest of it in an argument over a cab.

Mute and stiff, she let him walk her back toward his office, to the parking lot at the side of the building. His car was a dark maroon Mercedes convertible. He opened the door for her and closed it behind her after he'd put her in.

"Where to?" he asked from the driver's door. "Home?"

She nodded. She didn't trust her voice.

He didn't ask where she lived; it was obvious he knew the address. They drove the short distance in silence. When he made the turn onto her street, Ari straightened her shoulders and unclenched her teeth, rehearsing a civil thank-you and good-bye.

He pulled into a space across the street from her driveway and shut off the engine. When she looked at him, he was watching her, one wrist hooked on the top of the steering wheel as he turned toward her.

"Look," he said. "I apologize for not reacting the way you would have liked to the realization that my latest case carries some essential facts that all but guarantee I'll lose if I follow my client's plan. It's not a comfortable revelation for a lawyer to have. And I'm sorry your father got a rough deal, but I didn't send him to prison. I didn't invent the legal system that did. I just work in it, and yes, I do know how the system works. So if you want to fire me, do it on the basis of my competence, not on the basis of your personal distaste for the legal system. And I'd appreciate it if you'd do it in writing."

In the quiet that followed his speech, the ticking of the cooling engine sounded intrusive. He didn't move, nor did he make any attempt to keep her from simply getting out of the car and walking away. He wouldn't, she realized. His personal code didn't allow it. He wouldn't justify himself, he wouldn't coerce, and he wouldn't go beyond his own strict standard of persuasion to counteract her anger.

But it was enough. Her breath whooshed out in a long sigh. She didn't doubt his professional integrity. She'd never doubted it. And she'd known from the beginning, by instinct, that underneath his hard definitions of what he should be, he cared about what he did. Cared about what was right.

She glanced down at the leather-covered gear shift between them, then met his eyes again. "Would you like to come in?"

"Why?" he asked quietly. "You don't have pen and paper with you?"

She smiled. "My father's made spaghetti sauce. You'd be welcome to join us for supper."

He didn't move immediately. He was studying her, puzzling out the pieces he didn't know, turning that ferocious legal intelligence onto the problem of Ari Rossini and how he could contain her reactions, her values, in the bounds of what he defined as clear thinking.

He frowned, then let out a short, baffled huff of breath. His gaze was a little wary, slightly ironic. "Does this mean we're on a mutual first-name basis, Ms. Rossini?" he asked softly.

Feeling her pulse quicken, she forced herself to face what it meant, inviting him in, opening a part of her life to him. It seemed like a long time before she spoke. "Yes. That's what it means."

"Well, then." His mouth quirked in that crooked way he had of smiling when he wasn't sure he should allow himself to. "I guess you already know I'll say yes."

THREE

She'd surprised him again.

Why she'd done it didn't take much insight. She was preoccupied with her father's innocence, and her own. She wanted him to believe her.

Cord probed at that thought while he slammed the car door and pocketed his keys. Arianna crossed in front of the car and stopped beside him, waiting for him to move. Her expression silently asked why he hadn't. He took a step toward the house, and she turned to cross the street with him, then led the way up the wooden steps to the porch.

Sawdust smudged the back of her shirt, with another line across the worn seat of her jeans. Her hair caught on the edge of her collar, then, when she moved her head, it fell free, the strands of pale amber like silk against the flannel shirt. The contrast was extravagantly sensual, like black lace under denim jeans. His gaze flicked down again to the streak of sawdust. His body stirred in response.

Maybe Charlie was right. Maybe his temporary suspension of professional judgment had been spurred by hormones. There wasn't much doubt that his libido was a definite part of what she did to him.

Could do, he amended. It wasn't going to happen. Nothing was going to happen between them beyond a stray thought, a strictly private impulse. Cord Prescott wasn't given to either questionable ethics or stupidity.

Their footsteps across the wide porch rattled the dismantled railing stacked to one side of the entry, then were silenced by the sisal mat at the front door. The brass doorknob had been polished. She opened it without a key, stepped in ahead of him, and held the door to let him follow.

The house smelled of wax and spaghetti sauce and comfort. At the end of the entry hall, a lighted doorway beckoned.

"Pop? Hello?"

There was no answer. Family pictures lined the hallway. To his right Cord caught a glimpse of the living room. He had an impression of wood, polished, smooth, and meticulously refinished, the workmanship evident.

The kitchen was enormous. Her father, in chinos, blue-checked shirt, and a wool cap, with a linen towel tied around his waist, stood at the stove.

"Pop?" Arianna crossed the quarry-tiled floor and leaned over the pot to sniff appreciatively, then kissed her father on the cheek. "This is Cord Prescott," she said, glancing back to him. "He's staying for supper."

If her father was surprised at the abrupt invitation, he showed no sign of it. He stared across the kitchen at Cord in a frank assessment that wasn't asking for the details of an introduction.

"So you're Charlie Kent's partner. Prescott's son," he said.

The words held not even an attempt at conversational warmth, and Cord found himself straightening his shoulders, pulling his hands out of his pockets, aware of the challenge in Tomas Rossini's voice.

"That's right."

The older man studied Cord while he wiped his hands on his towel, drawing out the gesture. "You have the case all settled then?" he asked sarcastically.

The implication was clear: *You can take time off for socializing?*

Beside her father, Arianna made a slight gesture. "Pop—" she began in a tone that held rebuke, but Cord cut her off.

"No," he said, meeting the skeptical brown eyes. "It's a fair question. And the answer is no. We haven't settled the case. I'm here, as a matter of fact, because we haven't settled our first argument about it."

Thick eyebrows shot up, and Tomas flicked a questioning glance toward his daughter.

Arianna said nothing, but Cord could feel her tension in the straight line of her back.

He filled in the silence. "I want her to plead not guilty at the arraignment on Monday."

"Oh?" The lines in the older man's forehead creased. "Now you change your mind? And what does my daughter say to that?"

Cord looked at her directly. "She hasn't fired me yet."

"Should she?"

"That's up to her."

Arianna's father gave Cord a long, fierce look as he untied the linen towel around his waist. He flung the towel across the counter beside the stove. "Settle it, then," he said. "And if you want to eat here afterward, you can help cook." He reached for a package on the counter and thrust it into Cord's hands, then turned on his heel and stalked out of the kitchen.

Arianna watched his exit in shocked silence before she turned back to Cord. "I'm sorry."

"Don't be. Honesty's something I appreciate."

She shook her head, clearly embarrassed. "That kind of honesty?"

"Any kind I can get."

Her expression registered disbelief, but she let the comment pass. Her pale eyebrows drew together in puzzled assessment. "I guess you've had some honesty out of us today, then."

"I guess."

She crossed her arms, tucking her hands in, in a gesture he found telling: Casual, but with a hint of defensive anxiety. He knew before she spoke she was going to ask him something that was important to her.

"And do you believe people when they're honest with you, Mr. Prescott?"

The soft ivory skin over her cheekbones held a faint wash of color, hinting at a subtle emotion. He could almost feel her holding her breath, waiting for his answer, her dark eyes impossible to look away from.

The impulse to reassure her, to tell her *yes*, shocked him as much as it had in the holding cell where he'd met her.

God, he thought, when had he started accepting the truth of what he heard on faith instead of evidence?

The answer was swift and brooked no argument: He hadn't. The fact that Arianna Rossini had gotten past his professional guard was a phenomenon he couldn't explain.

Maybe it was the steady look. Or the unselfish motive behind her wish to plead nolo. Or the handcuff marks on her slender wrists.

He couldn't have said what it was that had gotten to him. But he knew for a fact he couldn't let it.

He let himself smile in mild apology, meeting her eyes. "I'm afraid skepticism is a necessary tenet of the profession, Arianna. Occupational hazard."

Whatever reaction she felt—dismay, disappointment, anger—she didn't show it with anything more than a slow release of her breath. She kept silent for the span of a few heartbeats, then unfolded her arms, her eyes still watching him. "You need to do some work with your hands, Mr. Prescott. Like carpentry. Or cooking. There's no dishonesty or cutting corners there—it shows in the finished product. You get used to that."

His gaze dropped to the package of fresh fettuccine noodles he held in his hands, as he considered her advice. As a cure for cynicism he wasn't sure whether he found it absurd or wise, but it was impossible anyhow. He looked back at Arianna, one eyebrow raised.

"You don't know how to cook pasta," she said. Her mouth curved into that slow smile that so enticed him. "Do you?"

He squeezed the package. "Is this a test?"

"I have a feeling you already passed the test."

Which test was that? he wondered. Pop's? Or hers? Or the one that would be played out around a conference table, where the terms would be Arianna's freedom? If he failed that one, she could lose her business, her livelihood, the work she loved. She could go to jail. An innocent woman could go to jail.

Cord swore silently, fighting back the protest that churned in his gut, denying the impulse that contradicted every tenet he'd lived half his life by.

"I think," he said, measuring out the words, "it would be wise to count the test results after they're in."

"Yes." She turned her head toward the doorway where her father had walked out. Slanting sunlight from the window sculpted the strong line of her jaw and the soft hollows of her throat. His gaze drifted down to the open collar of her shirt and the swell of her breasts. He wondered if she was wearing the cameo today, under the collar, against her skin.

"I really didn't mean to lead you into the lion's den when I asked you to come in. My father isn't usually like that."

"His daughter's not usually in this much trouble, I imagine."

"No. But still."

"Forget it, Arianna."

She considered, then, to his relief, said softly, "Okay."

He dropped his gaze again to the package in his hands. His fingers had dented the soft noodles. It wasn't professional concerns that had mutilated the fettuccine, he acknowledged wryly. It was a brickbat of undisciplined reaction that had no precedent in his experience.

The only smart thing to do was set her damn noodles down on the counter and walk out of there before he stayed so long, he'd have to examine just what the hell was going on between them. But he didn't do it.

"You're right about one thing," he told her. "I can't cook pasta. Not this kind. It's supposed to come in cardboard boxes with those little circles on the side for measuring how big a handful to throw in the pot."

"Here." She smiled slightly, reaching for the fettuccine. "I'll do it."

She got down a pan, filled it at the tap, turned on the burner.

Cord glanced away, shoving his hands into his pockets. Behind him was a tiled work counter with pots hanging over it. At the other end of the room a wooden trestle table flanked by tall chairs held a folded tablecloth, a handful of silverware, and an open bottle of wine. The table, finished to match the oak wainscoting and beveled cabinets, had been rubbed to a soft patina that spoke of loving care and meticulous workmanship. He wondered how much of it had been done by Arianna herself, her skilled hands shaping the wood with a craftsman's economy of movement, with the care she'd shown at her job that afternoon, her sense of the wood and her work unconsciously sensual.

The rhythmic *snick-snick-snick* of a knife on a chopping board brought his attention back to her. She was slicing celery, three stalks at a time, leaving swift, even triple rows of half-moons beyond the blade, which she tipped into a wooden salad bowl beside her elbow. With a flick of her hand she brushed her hair back from her shoulder, and the cascade caught the slanting sunlight. When she bent to wash lettuce under the tap, her shirt gaped between the second and third buttons, giving him a glimpse of peach-colored lace and a tiny satin bow.

He raised his eyes and found her looking at him, her expression candid and serious. "How much did Charlie tell you about my father's case?" she asked.

He leaned one hip against the counter and made himself relax. "Not much. We didn't talk about it in personal terms."

"Why not?"

"It's not a good idea for lawyers to get too involved in cases. And this was one he lost."

She pinned him with a probing look. "Does it bother you, personally, when you lose a case, Mr. Prescott?"

"I try not to let it."

And the client usually didn't ask, he thought. Or wonder.

Or want to plead guilty to a crime she didn't commit.

She reached for an onion and put it on the chopping board. The sweet-pungent smell of Spanish onion temporarily overpowered the simmering spaghetti sauce.

Cord made himself release the tension in his body and take a long breath, concentrating on the chopping board. "I'm surprised you don't cut off a finger," he said, his voice ironic. "Where'd you learn to do that?"

She grinned at him. "I'm good with my hands."

The image he'd been keeping at bay broke over him with the sudden force of a river in spring flood, irresistible as water: Her hands on his body, touching him the way she'd touched the wood that afternoon, caressing and pleasuring and speaking messages that could be expressed only through nerve and skin. His lips tracing the opening of her shirt. Frayed flannel and velvet skin and claimed intimacies. His hands tangled in her hair and his lips and tongue on her body, until she was the one whispering the words he was hearing in his head.

And I'm good with my mouth, babe. Let me show you.

Cord didn't move as his eyes met hers across the warm and fragrant kitchen. A forbidden image suggested itself and then coalesced between them, and he saw a startled awareness widen her eyes. He felt a surge of possessive satisfaction that he hadn't willed but couldn't control.

Logic told him what he was thinking had no possible reality. She couldn't share the fantasy. She hadn't read his mind, for God's sake. He hadn't spoken it.

Before he could finish the internal argument, she cut her finger and dropped the knife.

"Dammit!" The color in her face deepened. Surprise and annoyance dispelled the fantasy as she glanced toward him, examined her bleeding finger, then reached for a paper towel.

"Let me see." He caught her hand before she could wrap it up.

"It's nothing. Just careless." She squeezed the paper towel around it.

"Let me see," he said more sharply. He could feel her resistance, but she let him unwrap the paper towel and examine the cut. It wasn't deep, but the knife had been sharp and the wound was bleeding profusely. Cord wrapped it up again, pressing his fingers around the paper towel. "Have you got some sterile bandages, antiseptic?"

"Upstairs."

"Where?"

At the tense, clipped question she looked up at him, frowning. "It's just a cut. Not serious."

"So?" He made himself shrug. "You want to bleed all over your vegetables? You need a bandage."

"In my bathroom, upstairs."

The open door at the top of the stairs led into a separate apartment: Living room with floor-to-ceiling bookcases, kitchen, office crowded with neatly stacked blueprints on a long table.

Cord followed her into the bathroom at the end of the hall. He reached over her shoulder to the medicine cabinet and got out the bandages, then set them on the back of the sink, beside half a dozen tiny bottles of perfume. He took her hand again and held it toward a glass-shaded lamp on the wall flanked by framed photographs of formal Roman gardens. He was conscious, as she let him unwrap her finger and look at it, of the intimate confines of the small room and the personal act.

"It's still bleeding," he said. "Keep some pressure on it." He tore the paper off a gauze pad, applied it to the cut, and squeezed his fist around it. She gasped—a small sound that he felt rather than heard.

"I'm sorry." The words didn't begin to describe the stab of remorse that shot through him. He was putting on a Band-Aid, for Pete's sake, he told himself. She'd cut her finger with a kitchen knife, slicing vegetables.

But he'd distracted her. The symbolism didn't escape him.

She was too open. Too vulnerable.

She could be hurt.

"Dammit," she said softly.

Cord felt his jaw clench. He made himself let out a long breath. "Maybe you shouldn't trust me with your fingers."

"Maybe not." He glanced up and met serious brown eyes that held truths too unguarded to be safe.

She trusted too easily. Despite her teasing words, she left her hand willingly in his.

She'd leave her case in his hands too. He knew that, as surely as if he'd drawn up the legal contract. She would trust him with her life, her freedom . . . maybe, if he pushed it, her body, because she simply had no structure on which to hang the concept that trust was a policy followed only by those who couldn't afford lawyers.

He managed to apply antiseptic cream and the bandage in a neat, tight seal, but for a moment he wondered if his hands would shake.

She pulled her hand away from his when he'd finished, breaking the intimacy of contact, but not the charged, emotion-laden aura. Cord didn't move, standing beside the marble sink set in a hardwood counter, close enough to her to smell the faint scent of her hair. It was perfume, he realized. A subtle, light fragrance from one of the exotic bottles she kept on the back of her sink. Whenever she'd used it last, the scent had lingered in her hair, creating the intriguing, sensual illusion that the fragrance wafted from the images of the gardens framed on her wall.

"I've got blood on my shirt," she said with a slight, self-conscious shrug. "I'll go change it."

She left him in the bathroom and crossed to the opposite room. Cord glimpsed an Oriental rug and the edge of a white lace bedspread on a four-poster before she shut the door.

He ran a hand through his hair, staring at the closed door, picturing peach-colored lace against ivory skin until the surge of heat in his body forced him to turn away.

The table under the wall phone in the hallway

was littered with job memos, notes, and books propped facedown and open. He glanced over the slips of paper: Call Jack on the Hennings job. Return CD to Andy. Movies Saturday.

Andy. One of her crew. He wondered what her relationship was to him. And if he was the one she was going to the movies with on Saturday. None of his business, but it was pointless to deny the irrelevant and telling fact that he didn't like the possibility, and for reasons that had little to do with her case.

By the hallway window a set of shelves held seedlings in tiny square pots set into long trays. They were neatly labeled with names he'd never heard before. He had no interest in gardening. It took a certain kind of faith he didn't have. He touched one of the tiny leaves on a seedling marked *Nicotiana*.

She could be in prison when it was time to transplant it, if she was found guilty.

So get her a plea bargain that will keep her out. Sit down with the D.A. and make the deal.

Cord leaned against the doorframe to her office, staring at the plants, considering. Maybe he should hand it off to Charlie, take on one of Charlie's cases to balance the workload. Charlie was top-notch. Nobody could object to the switch.

But Charlie believed, if he was pushed, that she was guilty, just as he'd believed her father was guilty. To Charlie, "presumed innocent" was a legal fiction to be manipulated for the benefit of his clients.

Like Cord, he never asked about guilt or innocence. But in Charlie's case the reason wasn't professional restraint. It was because he already knew the answer. In Charlie's mind, everyone was guilty of something. *What* was just a technicality. And for reasons Cord couldn't begin to sort out, that final, cynical step over the line mattered.

Arianna Rossini had gotten under his guard, made him deal with feelings he hadn't acknowledged in years. He wasn't used to muddied instincts. Emotional involvement.

"If you flip the switch on the side of the shelves, the grow lights will come on," she said behind him.

He glanced back toward her. She'd changed into black jeans and a thigh-length green cotton sweater with the sleeves pushed up past her elbows and the single button at the neckline unfastened.

"What are all these?" he asked, sweeping his hand toward the shelves.

"Nicotiana, scented geraniums, some aromatic herbs."

"I've never heard of any of them."

She smiled. "They're unusual. I grow them for the way they smell. You can't always get them in nurseries."

He turned on the switch. The neon bulbs

flickered for a few seconds, then lit. "So you grow them yourself on the shelves here?"

"Until they get big enough to need transplanting. Then they go into the cold frame on the south side of the house, and I take over all the south windows for the ones that won't fit outside. By May they'll be crowding us out of the house."

His mouth quirked. "Seems like a lot of work for a few flowers that could all get plant rot or something and die on you."

Her eyebrows rose. "That's a pessimistic thing to say, Mr. Prescott."

"I'm a pessimistic man, Ms. Rossini."

She held his gaze for a moment, then looked down and crossed her arms in front of her, hugging her elbows.

"I can handle a plea bargain for you without implicating your father, Arianna," he said. "You'll have to give me some latitude, but I can give you my word I'll leave him out of it."

She studied him for a few seconds, then nodded, just a slight movement of her head.

Cord ran a hand through his hair, then looked back at her and grinned.

"I knew your father," she said unexpectedly. "I met him when I was fourteen."

He let the grin fade, not sure of the direction of her thoughts.

"He wasn't like Charlie," she went on. "Your father scared me."

"Yeah," Cord said. "He scared me, too, when I was fourteen."

"But not when you were older?"

"No. Not since I figured out he was doing it on purpose."

"On purpose." She studied him. "And when was that?"

"Not long after I turned fourteen."

"I can't imagine a father who would want to scare his child on purpose."

"Can't you? You must have a limited imagination."

"Maybe I don't want to imagine it."

"Maybe your father saves all his scare tactics for the men you bring home."

She blinked, startled, and Cord cursed the urge that had prompted him to make such a personal comment.

She didn't take offense, though. She uncrossed her arms and pushed her sleeves farther up, lifting her chin in the way he was beginning to recognize. "He scared the last one," she said directly. "My fiancé. We never got around to setting a date, and I finally realized there was a reason. He didn't want to take on Pop as well as me. He didn't understand my feelings about family."

Cord thought about saying *I'm sorry*, conventional sympathy, but killed the words before they were out. Maybe her honesty was catching. Or maybe he wasn't quite that much of a hypocrite.

"If he didn't understand that, then you're probably right. Better to figure it out beforehand."

"Yes." She sounded surprised.

Or maybe it was his own surprise. He didn't usually say things quite so evocative of simple sentimentality. That was for his witnesses. *Your honor, I'm trying to establish the character of the witness here, so the defense can rest its case and get on to more immediate concerns with the accused.*

"Do you have any other family?" she asked.

"No," he said. Then, gruffly, "Just Charlie. He's almost family."

She held his gaze for a moment, her eyes wide. With amusement he realized what she felt for his family-free status was sympathy.

She started to say something, but was cut off by her father's irate voice from the bottom of the stairs.

"Arianna! What are you doing up there? You left the pasta boiling over!"

"Oh." She muttered something under her breath, shot Cord a rueful look, and turned toward the stairs. "Take it off the burner, will you?" she called down. "I forgot it."

"It's off." Pop scowled at Cord as he followed Ari downstairs. The message was clear, Cord thought with a touch of wry humor. Pop didn't trust lawyers, and his mistrust had just been proven again. Bring a lawyer into the house and the pasta overcooks.

"My fault," he said to Pop. "We needed a medic, not a lawyer. My first-aid skills are rusty."

"I cut my finger," Arianna said as they followed the older man toward the kitchen.

He grunted. "Bad?"

She smiled. "I've had worse troubles."

Pop glanced toward the bandage on her hand, then shifted his gaze to Cord. His thoughts, it was clear, were on his daughter's case. "You have worse troubles now," he told her.

In the big kitchen the table had been set with a green cloth, silverware, salad, and three steaming plates of pasta. Beside the bottle of wine was a cheese grater and a loaf of bread, four-pointed, as if two loaves had been tied together before baking.

Cord took the chair opposite Arianna, reached for his napkin, and silently calculated the minutes it would take for them to get through dinner and express decently civil parting remarks. He had the napkin on his lap before he realized Pop was eyeing him, his hands folded, his elbows propped beside his plate.

"We say grace," Arianna murmured. "My mother always insisted on it."

Grace, Cord thought. They were about to say grace. He put his napkin back beside the plate, trying to remember the last time he'd sat at a table where someone blessed the food.

Pop muttered something Cord couldn't understand. When he looked up, Arianna poured

Pop's glass full of wine before she filled Cord's and then her own.

The food was excellent, the wine less so, the conversation all but nonexistent. Pop's animosity was borne of worry, Cord knew, and Pop had cause for worry. Their differences weren't going to be settled over dinner. The fact that no one was pretending they were made the tension just barely tolerable.

The bread was passed around without a basket. Pop watched Cord break off a corner, then dip it into the dish of seasoned olive oil in front of his place.

"It's Bolognese bread," he told Cord. "Arianna's mother was from Bologna." Cord nodded, and the older man added, "She died eight years ago."

It would have been when Pop was in jail. Cord assimilated that fact without comment but with no doubt as to the intent of the exchange. Pop had reason to be bitter. The fact that he was only gruff and distant explained something about Ari's devotion to him.

"It's good, Pop," she said. "The bread."

Her softly voiced comment didn't smooth the unspoken crosscurrents eddying around the table. She glanced at Cord, and when he met her eyes, she offered a slight smile of apology. Cord found himself studying her as they ate.

She'd brought him there to show him how it was between her and her father. *Let me show you,* she was challenging him, *what you plan to use for a sacrifice.*

It had worked, far more effectively than any stipulation she could have given him about the handling of her case. Her father's life had been impoverished beyond measure by his charge, his conviction. Cord could well imagine that seeing his daughter suffer the same fate would kill him.

He shut his eyes for a moment, feeling the weight of that thought, letting his fork rest on his plate beside the excellent pasta he had no appetite for. When he opened his eyes, Arianna was watching him, making no attempt to eat, her own fork loose in her fingers.

"You probably have things to attend to," she said.

He nodded. "I'll start with the police file and some calls to the statehouse. Monday I'll want to start checking your office records. I'll want to go back a few years." He didn't say *to your father's case*, but no one missed the implication.

Her throat worked, and she shot a quick glance toward her father.

"I'll need your help, Ari."

Pop wiped his mouth, then threw his napkin down beside his plate. "I thought it went the other way, lawyer," he said. "My daughter needs *your* help."

"It goes both ways," Cord told him. "We'll be working together on this."

"But my daughter," Pop said, glancing toward her, "is the one who will pay if you lose."

There wasn't any answer to that, and Cord didn't offer one.

"Someone did this to my daughter. Someone framed her."

". . . Who?" Cord said into the tight silence.

"I don't know that. You find out."

There was no answer to that demand, either. It was time to leave. Cord pushed back from the table and stood. "Thank you for the meal," he said to Pop. "I'm sorry the occasion doesn't do it justice."

The older man rose from his chair and faced Cord across the table, his fists planted beside his plate, his expression fierce. "I don't want your thanks for the meal, *Lawyer*. I want you to keep my daughter out of prison."

The challenge, flung down like a glove, charged the air between them with new tension. For a moment no one moved.

Cord broke the frozen impasse, pushing his chair under the table with careful control. "That's what I intend to do," he said.

He walked back through the hall and let himself out.

Ari was behind him. Her hurried footsteps brought her to the door before he could close it. She stepped out onto the porch with him and shut the door behind them, then waited until he turned to face her.

"Cord," she said softly. "Thank you . . . for listening to Pop without getting angry . . . for preserving his dignity."

"No thanks necessary. Lawyers aren't supposed to get angry. Unless it's a courtroom performance."

"But he was rude. I apologize for him."

Her eyes showed every nuance of concern and vulnerability. "You don't have to apologize, either," he said brusquely. "Your father has concerns. He expressed them. Fair enough. He has no reason to trust me."

She shook her head. "He does have reason to trust you. You're a man who can be trusted."

The dusky evening light defined her face in simplistics: The planes and angles under the ivory skin, the deepening color of emotion across her cheeks, her eyes dark and fervent. He countered the effect she had on him with a huff of laughter. "He doesn't know that, Ari. You don't know it, either. You have no proof."

"No, I suppose I don't. None that would hold up in a court of law at least." She didn't look away. Her steady gaze burned into him with an intensity that stirred places too deep to recognize. "I'll put it this way, then," she said. "I trust you."

He was shaking his head before she finished. "Ari, I can't give—"

Her fingertips touched his lips, silencing him with the intimate shock of flesh against flesh.

"Don't," she said softly. "Don't do that to yourself. I trust you."

He lifted his hand and circled her wrist. His intention, if he could have framed it, was to take her hand away, but he didn't do it. He held her fingers against his mouth while a breath of wind stirred her hair, touching it the way he wanted to touch it. Then, without anything as coherent as thought, he raised her hand and brought his mouth to the inside of her wrist, where the mark from the handcuffs was still faintly visible. Her skin was warm and sweet and soft, and beneath his mouth he could feel the rapid, erotic rhythm of her pulse.

The muscles in his gut clenched tight, and the blood surging through his veins stirred a response too graphic to deny. Her eyes told him she knew it, but she said nothing, made no move to act on the urges that spun between them, or to deny the force of that bond.

Long seconds later she pulled her hand away, turned toward the door, and let herself in.

Cord stayed where he was, staring at the lighted rectangle of etched Victorian glass, watching her blurred silhouette grow smaller as she walked down the hall.

The taste of her lingered on his tongue long after she'd disappeared.

FOUR

Rossini, Tomas.

Cord stared at the glowing green letters until they blurred, then he rubbed his fingers across his eyes and pinched the bridge of his nose. *Tomas, without an H.* Even after he'd figured out how to spell it, the file didn't tell him anything.

The muted sound of a closing door could have been a comment on his progress with the case.

In the dark, empty office suite the footsteps crossing the reception room were just audible. Cord swiveled his chair around as the footsteps grew closer. Charlie appeared around the edge of the doorway, paused there, then leaned against the doorjamb and crossed one foot in front of the other, scuffing his Italian leather toe on the threshold. He was dressed in evening clothes, headed, no doubt, for one of the high-rent functions he patronized. Charlie liked the good life.

"You planning to sleep with that computer to-night?" Charlie asked, surveying the scattered papers, discarded sweatshirt, empty plastic containers from take-out food. "Because if you think you're going to get any satisfaction, I'd suggest a hell of a lot more romance in your approach."

Cord's mouth quirked. "Maybe I'll try it. Couldn't work any worse than what I've been doing."

"What *have* you been doing?" Charlie took a couple of steps into the computer room and leaned over Cord's shoulder to read the screen. "Tomas Rossini?" He shook his head. "I don't keep files on cases that old."

"So I see."

Charlie shrugged and leaned one elbow on the computer, making his jacket gape over his white dress shirt. "You want information about it? Ask me. I'm a fountain."

Cord frowned. "That was a lot of years ago, Charlie. I don't expect you to remember the details."

"Tomas was a friend of mine," Charlie said softly. "I remember the details. What do you want to know?"

"Who was he working for when he was indicted?"

Charlie picked up one of the printouts, rummaged in his coat pocket for the pen he always kept there, and scribbled the words on the back of the paper. "Here."

Cord took it from him.

"An operation called Wilson Graphics. Went bankrupt a few years ago. And Rossini's crew. None of 'em are still in the area."

Cord studied the paper, frowning.

"I'll tell you something, though," Charlie added. "Wilson Graphics had a couple of backers who lost some money when they went belly-up. One of them was Frank Oslund."

"The D.A.?"

"You got it. He wasn't with the prosecutor's office then. He was just a slick junior partner in some two-bit law firm, looking to find an out for his ambitions. You can bet he wasn't happy about losing his investment. And he was pretty sure Tomas Rossini was to blame for it."

"How about you?"

Charlie tapped his fingers once on the top of the computer. "I went to high school with Tomas. We were on the soccer team together. That was a tough case to lose."

Cord said nothing.

"I'll tell you this, though," Charlie went on. "Oslund would be willing to believe Tomas Rossini was behind this one too."

"She won't agree to using that."

"No," Charlie said, as if the answer was the one he'd expected. "Well, then, your girl's on her own, partner."

On her own.

A sensation that was becoming familiar twisted

in his gut. "Not quite," he murmured, glancing up at Charlie. "She's got a lawyer."

The computer hummed a solitary comment. Charlie's gaze didn't move from Cord's face. "Where're you goin' with this, Cord?" he asked finally.

"Conference. Plea bargain. Whatever it takes to cut a deal with the D.A."

"No. I don't mean legally. I mean personally." He flattened his palm on the top of the computer, assessing his partner. "You involved with this woman?"

Cord leaned back in his chair, reaching for his coffee cup to cover his reaction to the question. "You think I'm sleeping with a client, Charlie?"

"Are you?"

Cord made himself stare at his coffee, bringing his quick flare of anger under control with the ruthless, blunt reminder that Charlie's comment wasn't so far off the mark.

But it *was* off. In ways that made his reaction to a partner's probing question a hell of an act to explain.

Cord's fingers curled around the cup, holding it the way he'd held her wrist outside her front door.

Fragile. Strong. Passionate in her belief.

On her own.

The thought reached down inside his gut and lodged there as if it wasn't going to let go. He could still feel the delicate bone structure of her wrist, belied by the strength and skill in her hands. He could have traced the shape of her face from memory. Boyish jaw, pale eyebrows, magnificent dark eyes.

She had no knowledge of the persuasive power she could wield with her face and her body. She used them the way she spoke, with a direct and forthright transparency too real to be manipulative.

He shut his eyes for a moment, letting out his breath between his clenched teeth. *An honest client.* Maybe that was why she got to him. He didn't have any professional framework to fit her into. She didn't belong in the same system that had spawned a lawyer like Cord Prescott.

He looked up at his partner. "I'm not getting involved with her, Charlie," he said.

The older man nodded, satisfied. "Good. Then I don't have to tell you what you already know. You get mixed up with her, and you'll put yourself on a fast track to self-destruction. You can get burned with this one, Cord. If you're lookin' for a woman, this one is not a good bet."

Cord couldn't leave it. "And why is that?"

"You mean aside from the fact she's a client? Aside from the fact that this law firm hired her and she was workin' for us when the whole mess came down? Aside from the fact that our esteemed district attorney has a bone to pick with her father and wouldn't mind using Arianna Rossini to do it? And incidentally wouldn't mind making the best defense attorney in the city look like a fool?"

"Yeah," Cord said. "Aside from that."

Charlie gave him a faint, resigned smile and shook his head, then let the smile die into something grimmer. "Because the chances are too good she's going to jail."

The anteroom of the Worcester Superior Court smelled of dusty asphalt tile and old wood. To Arianna, standing in the middle of the room, accosted by the babble of voices and the feelings of tense urgency and hopeless resignation, the smell was the only thing familiar.

Pop had done this, she told herself, alone, refusing to let his family come with him to the trial. He'd wanted to protect them, he'd said. It hadn't worked. The family had been torn apart anyway— her sister Rosa denying it, unable to face the truth, their mother becoming silent and distant. And now Pop, bitter and angry and still unreconciled.

Standing there, one fist pressed against her stomach, she understood something about why he'd fought so hard. Maybe the fighting had made it easier for him. He'd faced his accusers with righteous indignation.

She'd chosen instead to put her trust in a lawyer who hadn't asked if she was guilty or innocent. Who'd implied it didn't matter. Who wouldn't let himself believe in innocence, or righteous anger. Or trust.

She closed her eyes, conjuring up an image sharp enough to shut out the sounds and sights and smells. An image of intense gray eyes, dark hair, wide mouth with an ironic smile. The way he put himself at ease with all this. He had power in this system of courts and prisons that she could barely imagine having. He would use it for her.

But it would cost him something. She knew that.

The teenager who had stood up to his father's scare tactics had paid a price in lost innocence. Her case—the debt he owed to Charlie—was part of that price.

She didn't want to be part of any price he had to pay.

The realization wove its way through her as an inarguable truth. For the space of two missed heartbeats she examined that fact, sorting out her reaction, understanding what she wanted. Cord's smile. His trust. The touch of his mouth on her wrist. The promise of something that took her breath away.

She must have made some sound. A policeman holding the elbow of a handcuffed prisoner glanced toward her curiously. She made herself look back, meeting the eyes of jailer and prisoner with the same level appraisal, but her fists were closed so tightly, her nails dug into her palms.

"You're early."

She jumped at the sound of his voice. Cord moved toward her from the doorway of the anteroom, walking with the loose, casual stride of a man who traversed these surroundings without thought. Something curled tight in her chest, like the shoot inside a seed, ready to burst it.

"I thought we were going to meet at ten o'clock," he said.

"Yes. But I came early. I wanted to have a chance to . . . get used to things."

He studied her, unsmiling. "Didn't work, did it?" he said grimly. "Come on. We'll walk down to the coffee machine. It's in the basement."

Her stomach lurched. "I don't think I want coffee."

"You certainly don't want the stuff that comes out of this machine. Come on, we'll get you a soda."

He'd already started walking. He pulled open the heavy glass door to the stairway and held it for her.

She needed that certitude right now. With only a small hesitation she followed to the stairs and went ahead of him through the door. It swung shut behind them, dimming the sound of the voices in the anteroom.

He walked beside her down the stairs, his briefcase brushing her skirt, distracting her in a way she shouldn't have permitted. But she needed the distraction. Her awareness of his shoulder next to hers, his hand gripping the briefcase at the

level of her wrist, his loose, athletic strides made
her breath catch and her pulse beat with something besides anxiety—something she needed as
much as his experience with the law.

The machines were around a corner from the
stairwell, at one side of a dingy, linoleum-floored
lunchroom with Formica tables and plastic chairs.
Cord fed change into one of the slots, then turned
back to her with a can of soda in his hand.

"Thank you."

"You're welcome. You look"—he flicked a
glance down the length of her navy blue wool suit,
then met her eyes again, his mouth curving in a
slight smile—"like a lawyer."

He startled her into an unexpected laugh, but
his own smile faded into a more serious expression
as he watched her.

"No. Amend that," he said. "You look like an
honest woman."

Startled again, she gave him a quizzical look,
half convinced he meant the comment as a joke.
His eyes were level on her face, though, and there
was no hint of laughter in his softly spoken adden-
dum.

"It becomes you."

She didn't register the meaning of the words
right away—what they said about her and what
they said about the self-proclaimed cynic who
spoke them.

She clutched the can of soda in both hands and

made herself take a long, deep breath. "This is harder than I thought it would be."

"It's just routine, Arianna. You enter your plea, the judge explains that you can waive your right to a jury trial and appear before the judge only. We decline that right, and he sets a trial date. We say, 'Thank you, Your Honor,' and walk out. Five minutes in court."

She nodded, and managed a sketchy smile. "You've done this before."

"More times than I can count."

She was briefly silent. "And every time, you were defending a client whose life was being torn apart, one way or another."

"Yes."

She looked away from him, but something that had flickered across his face stayed with her, touching the part of her that wasn't consumed by her own private trial. When she looked back, his expression was schooled into polite concern. Whatever she'd seen was buried again, pushed down into the storage bin he used for any feelings that could make him vulnerable.

"How do you do it?" she asked softly.

"I do it well, that's how. I'm good at my job. You can trust that."

It wasn't what she'd meant, and he knew it, but Ari didn't protest the deliberate misinterpretation. He'd called her an honest woman, but he wouldn't hear the same about himself. It was easier for him to give grace than to take it, she thought.

"We'll go up now," he said. "The docket is running early this morning. Anything you need to ask me, at any time, you can. That's your right."

In court. Not in person. The private thought carried a measure of pain she hadn't expected, like the sting of an insect she hadn't seen coming.

I'm a pessimistic man, he'd said Saturday, but his fingers had touched the leaf of a seedling with such care, she'd thought of it as tenderness.

She heard the same self-censure here, and she didn't know how to respond to it.

He held out his hand for the empty can. She gave it to him, then followed him up the stairs, across the deserted anteroom, and in through the heavy oak doors to the courtroom.

The room was half full—occupied by many of the same people she'd seen in the anteroom, seated now on ornately carved dark wood seats. Behind the elaborate bench a black-robed judge— the one Cord had told her was tough on cases like hers—presided over the courtroom.

Ari stiffened involuntarily, fighting a twinge of panic. Cord's hand touched her back, and he walked her up the center aisle to an empty row of seats. The small gesture was correct, polite, but just casual enough to convey an impression of assurance. The bailiff nodded as he caught Cord's eye. A few heads turned. A few more nods.

She felt herself relaxing in response to the

confidence he projected. *He was good at this*, she told herself, clinging to the thought.

He touched her shoulder to get her attention, then nodded toward the front row of seats, where a heavyset blond man glanced back at Cord, his expression wary and faintly antagonistic. "The district attorney," Cord said, near her ear. "Frank Oslund."

She pulled her eyes away from the icy blue gaze of the district attorney and glanced toward Cord, questioning.

"He's expecting a no contest plea," Cord told her. "He won't be pleased with this. Don't let his reaction rattle you."

The D.A. was staring at Cord, and as he took in Cord's focused intent, his expression grew more grim. With a trace of outrage, he snapped his gaze to Arianna.

She could read the resentment and anger all the way across the room. He'd seen something in Cord's eyes that he took as a warning, and he didn't like it. He'd counted on an easy conviction, a guilty plea. She felt a chill snake down her back and settle like cold lead in her stomach, where panic shivers were gathering again.

Cord leaned forward, resting his elbows on his knees, abruptly cutting off her view of Oslund and shielding her from the man's angry glare.

Ari let out a long breath and tried to distract herself with a desperate assessment of her surroundings. The room was Victorian, the woodwork heavily carved, in need of renovation. A water stain angled down from one high window. The frame had warped from the moisture. An old patina of cracks fanned out across the surface of the wood.

Her father had probably seen the same damage, she thought with a trace of black irony. He might have assessed the cost of repairs just as she was doing, keeping his mind occupied. Had Charlie protected him from the stare of his accuser? Would he have, or was that small, protective gesture unique to Cord Prescott, despite his claims of cynicism?

When the clerk announced their case and Cord touched her arm, she jumped. With hard-fought balance she managed to walk steadily toward the front of the room, aware of the stares of all the strangers behind her. She stood without moving in front of the judge.

The charges were familiar. She listened stoically, her eyes level on the judge's face. In the case of the Commonwealth of Massachusetts versus Arianna Rossini: Fraud, misrepresentation with intent to defraud, embezzlement of 105,000 dollars in connection with the project she had undertaken at 75 Chestnut Street to renovate a building of historical significance.

When he was finished there was a silence long enough to make Cord lean toward her, but his prompt wasn't necessary. She raised her chin and said, "Not guilty."

Oslund slapped his file against his leg with enough force to make Arianna snap her head around toward him. The D.A. glared at Cord, then spun on his heel and stalked out.

"I guess he's not ready to talk," Cord muttered into her ear. The judge set the trial date.

Cord didn't touch her as they went out. In silence they walked past the clerk and through the heavy doors, across the anteroom, and down the courthouse steps.

The courthouse lawn was greening in patches of struggling grass. Ari stopped halfway across it and looked down, studying her navy blue pumps. As if it were a careful decision, she slipped her feet out of them and bent to pick them up, standing in her stockings on the damp grass.

"Isn't this illegal?" she asked him. "Trespassing on the courthouse lawn?"

As he'd watched her take off her shoes, Cord had felt his mouth tip up at the corners. Whatever he'd expected from her after her tense composure in the courtroom, it wasn't this gentle humor. His own shoulders, he realized, were still knotted. He shrugged, loosening the knots. "Yes, but I don't think they'll prosecute."

"Good. I wouldn't want you to go to jail."

"Neither would I."

She smiled at him, briefly.

"Here's where I'm supposed to say, 'That wasn't so bad after all, was it?' But I have a feeling

I'd be missing some essential point if I said it this time."

She shook her head, with another sketchy smile. "Some things maybe it's better to miss."

"Not when I'm counsel and you're the client."

Her eyes widened in surprise at the sharpness of his tone. He aimed another silent curse at himself. It wasn't what she needed to hear. It was what he needed to remember. "Ari," he said more softly, "why don't you tell me what's happening here?"

When she looked at him again, her dark, golden-lashed eyes caught his gaze and held it. "You don't mean with the embezzlement charges, do you? You mean what I'm thinking."

He thought about denying it, but it hadn't been phrased as a question. "Yes."

She started walking again, across the checkered grass, in her stocking feet. "It was that question—*How do you plead?*"

"You mean, not guilty?"

"No." She shook her head. "The question. *How do you plead?* Like when I asked you how you do it, handle all those court cases, and you said you do it well."

He submitted to her serious scrutiny in silence.

After a moment she looked away. "The night before my father was convicted, he finally realized the jury wasn't going to deliver a not-guilty verdict. He took me aside and explained it. I was fifteen, but I pleaded with him like a little girl not to leave us. Not to go to prison, as if he had some choice in it. He promised me he'd come back. He told me to take care of my mother." She sighed. "I gave my mother a hard time after he left. I was fifteen, rebellious, resentful. It took me three years to realize it wasn't his fault. And when he did come back, my mother wasn't there to welcome him."

Something painful tightened in his chest. Something that didn't belong in a lawyer's repertoire of reactions. He shoved his free hand into his pants' pocket, too sharply aware of the urge to touch her, to hold her as he would have if she were still fifteen and frightened and faced with the stark, ruthless fact that life was unfair and its victims were whoever happened to be in the way.

He didn't want her to know that, he realized, and was stymied by the illogical reaction.

"You were there for him," he said. "You were still there when he came home."

She glanced at him. "I was running his business. He had a lot of loyal customers. They gave their loyalty to me, because I'm his daughter."

"I think you've earned it, Ari."

"I have now. It's been a few years. I've established a reputation. I've done . . . honest work."

She stopped and shook her head. "That was what he held on to. Honesty. This—for me—seems so unreal, so . . . *staged*. Pleading not guilty and thinking, I'll face this same judge later and tell him no, I've changed my mind. We've made a deal, and now I'm guilty." She looked away again. "That will be worse than today, won't it?"

"I don't know," he said. "It isn't, for most of my clients. You'll know what's going to happen then. There won't be any more uncertainty."

"Yes. I'll have a deal."

It was the first trace of bitterness he'd heard from her, and it wrenched at something in him that protested the wrongness of that tone.

"You won't go to jail," he said.

"What will I have to do?"

"Pay a fine. Make restitution."

"And admit I'm guilty."

There was no answer to that, nothing he could say to lighten the weight, to ease the silence that had become grating. He knew his role in this case. He was too good a lawyer not to know it.

With something like detached bafflement he heard himself say, almost casually, "We could take it to trial."

A flare of response darkened her eyes. He watched the thoughts chase across her expressive face: Disbelief, anger, pain.

He suppressed a succinct curse, regretting the senseless impulse that never should have been spoken.

"No."

Her voice caught on the one word.

"I can't do that, Cord," she went on, stronger now. "I can't do it to my father. You've met him. You know that!"

"Yes, I do."

"I thought you understood." Her anguished eyes beseeched something he couldn't take in. Something that hurt. He started walking again, across the lawn toward the sidewalk.

"Cord?"

"It's not my business to understand, Ari. It's my business to dispose of this case to your satisfaction. Which I will do."

"You think I'm doing the wrong thing, though, don't you?"

"Of course not."

She stopped at the edge of the lawn, visibly upset. "But *you* want to take it to trial. You want a trial. You want an acquittal."

"That's not up to me."

"I don't mean you want it as a lawyer. I mean—" She broke off, leaving the dangerous words unspoken.

"I *am* a lawyer," he said, too sharply. "This is a case. You're the one who has to live with the outcome."

"Cord." She put her hand on his arm, not lightly, but with a strong, sure grip, pulling him around to face her. Over the perfect bone structure of her cheeks and jaw, her skin was rich ivory, her eyes dark and enormous and full of complex feelings: Frustration, anger, determination . . . and a glimmer of rebellious, passionate fire he recognized, with a jolt, as sensual awareness.

For a long moment he wondered if his self-control would hold.

"Yes," she said finally. Her voice had a low, husky catch that spoke directly to the surge of blood in his veins. "I'm the one who has to live with the outcome. I know what the facts are. And the dangers."

Cord told himself to move away from her. He could just picture District Attorney Oslund walking out of the courthouse and seeing his prime suspect locked in an embrace with her defense attorney on the front lawn of the courthouse.

"But I'm making it hard for you, aren't I?" Ari went on. "Asking you to plea-bargain. To compromise. To do something you don't want to do."

"You have a right to ask me to plea-bargain, Arianna. I'm a lawyer. That's what I do."

A smear of emotion stained her cheeks.

"Forget it, Ari," he said, more softly. "What I want doesn't matter. What you want does. I'm your lawyer. That's the relationship we have."

She studied his face, her breaths coming more quickly than they should have. They both knew that what he'd just said wasn't true.

She didn't attempt to dissemble. She lifted her chin a fraction of an inch and confronted him. "Maybe I care what you want."

He didn't let himself move.

"Maybe I care what you want not just as a lawyer, but as a person. As a man."

"Arianna . . ."

"I just don't know what you're going to do about it."

He'd underestimated her again. Her determination, her straightforwardness, her courage in the face of the truth.

I just don't know what you're going to do about it.

The answer was obvious. She was his client. He was her attorney, defending her on a charge of embezzlement that would need every scrap of objectivity he could muster. *Nothing* was what he was going to do about it. That was the only possible answer he could give.

But in a sudden, unplanned movement, he reached for her and cupped the back of her neck with one hand. "Neither do I," he said gruffly. At her throat, he could see the tiny, quick beat of her pulse. His hand tightened around her nape, his fingers threading into her hair, pulling her closer and tipping her head up until their mouths were just an inch away from touching. In trancelike slow motion his thumb traced the line of her jaw and the delicate cord of her neck.

She whispered something that wasn't quite a word. Cord didn't catch it, but the small movement of her lips mesmerized him. He felt a surge of energy so focused, it seemed to fuse them to-

gether even across the space that still separated
their mouths. He knew what she'd be like: Giving,
sure of herself, passion showing in her face, her
voice breathless as she told him what she wanted.

And he knew, too, that he wanted it as well, as
much as he'd ever wanted anything in his life. Her
passion, her honesty, her loyalty. He wanted all of
it, no matter what it cost. No matter who it hurt.
And there was no way in hell he would stop himself once he started.

It took every ounce of his will to release her.
When he dropped his hand, he shoved it into his
pocket and took a step away from her, staring out
across the street, seeing nothing.

She made no sound at all until, finally, he
heard her let out her breath. He sensed her bending to put on her shoes, hitch her purse strap over
her shoulder.

"Do you need a ride home?" he asked gruffly.

"No."

"I'll call you after I've checked the evidence
the D.A. is holding."

She nodded, then, with the same dignity she'd
had in the courtroom, she turned and walked away
from him.

Cord stayed where he was until he could no
longer hear her footsteps on the concrete sidewalk.

It took him a while to realize he was staring at
the little park beside the courthouse. The willow

tree was just starting to bud, looking greener than it should have in the pale brown and gray landscape. The stray thought that ran through his mind was so odd, it made him shake his head.

That spring growth must hurt like hell.

FIVE

Cord had said he'd call her when he examined the evidence in the D.A.'s file. Logic told her that staring at the phone wouldn't make it ring, but Ari couldn't seem to bring herself to do anything else.

Pop, puttering in the kitchen downstairs, was baking coffee cake. She knew it was a silent offer for her to come down and sit with him, but she couldn't face him yet with an eye-to-eye report on the arraignment: The plea, the dealing, the venomous outrage of the district attorney before he'd stalked out of the courtroom.

. . . Or the grass of the courthouse lawn under her feet, the bright, cool sun on her face, Cord Prescott with his hand threaded into her hair, refusing to kiss her.

She reached out to touch the fragile leaf of a basil seedling in the window box.

He thought he was going to hurt her. He was probably right.

What shook her to the depths of her soul, though, was the part he wouldn't admit. He could be hurt too.

She closed her eyes for a moment, sending up some silent, wordless prayer.

The trill of the phone startled her as if a hand had tapped her on the shoulder. She jumped, then wiped her palms on her jeans before she reached for the receiver.

It took her a moment to realize it was not Cord's voice that answered her greeting.

"Is Victor, Arianna. With news not so good."

Victor? Her head carpenter's soft-spoken voice was not usually accented. An alarm trickled down her spine. "What is it, Victor?"

"Andy. He's been arrested. He's at the police now. The station."

"The *police station?* Why?"

"He violated the order, from the police, to stay away from the Chestnut Street job," Victor told her. "He was over there, and the cops caught him."

Incredulous, she clutched the phone and muttered, "What was he doing there?"

In the slight hesitation that followed, she could hear the interrupted cadence of work sounds—the rest of her crew, minus their apprentice, pretending not to listen to Victor.

"The D.A. was here this morning, Arianna.

That guy, Oslund. Talking about . . . some more charges."

She opened her mouth, but no sound came out. The coffee she'd swallowed churned in her stomach. "What charges?"

"He was talking like he knew something we didn't. Said he had evidence over to the other job that you were . . . that you were planning an accident over there to cover things up. That you deliberately crossed some electrical wires."

"*What?*"

"There could've been a fire, he said. He was tryin' to tell us we'd better confess what we know or we'd get implicated along with you."

Arianna leaned back against the wall for support.

"Well, you know Andy," Victor went on, sounding apologetic. "He's got a bad temper. He clammed up when the D.A. was here, but after the guy left Andy just . . . walked out. Said he was going to check out that story for himself."

"It isn't true."

"No. We know it's not true."

Holding the phone to her ear, she crossed her other arm over her stomach. She felt like she'd been kicked. Andy, her apprentice carpenter, had gone to the Kent & Prescott job site, against police orders—and hers. "Oh, Lord," she murmured, the word halfway between a prayer and a curse. "What did he think—?" She cut off the sentence abruptly.

"I didn't know what to do about bail or what-ever," Victor said uncertainly.

"I'll take care of it," she said.

"I don't like to stick this on you."

"It's okay, Victor. I'm the boss."

"Yeah . . . well, I'm sorry," Victor muttered. "I shouldn't have let him go. He's just a dumb kid. I should've . . ." His voice trailed off.

She had to swallow around another lump in her throat. "No. You did the right thing, Victor. Just . . . run the job for me, okay?"

The mahogany and glass door of the law office opened onto a pale-gray-carpeted reception area occupied by a receptionist who sat behind a computer terminal.

Ari shut the door behind her, listening to the quiet click of brass hardware and the whisper of the thick Oriental carpet under her sneakers. Everything about the classically appointed law office was expensive and well crafted. Made to reassure and impress, like the trappings of a courtroom—the bench, the rail, the gavel. Telling an observer the law's justice could be trusted.

"Can I help you?"

The receptionist's gaze flicked just once over the jeans and unbuttoned suit jacket Ari wore, but she was too well trained to display surprise.

"I'd like to see Cord Prescott. I'm a client. Arianna Rossini."

"I'll see if he's available." The woman got up and walked behind her desk toward an archway that led to a corridor of closed doors.

Ari watched her disappear through one of them.

This was Cord's world: Expensive offices, trained staff, the click and whir of computers from beyond another arched entry.

He'd spoken a profound truth on the courthouse lawn, when he'd said he was a lawyer. It was what he did. His life.

It was what they were to each other: Lawyer and client.

She leaned back against the door, her hands clasped behind her on the brass doorknob, her eyes closed as if she could shut out that harsh reality.

When she opened them again, Cord was standing in the doorway to the reception area.

He'd taken off his jacket, loosened his tie, and unhooked the top button of his shirt. His hands were in his pockets, his hair disheveled, his mood easy to read. He didn't have any illusions that this was a social visit.

"Arianna," he said, his voice neutral, uninflected, carefully free of either apprehension or annoyance at what he must know was a trouble call.

She straightened. "I'm sorry to interrupt you," she said. "But I have a problem I need your help with."

He nodded, then gestured with one hand toward the archway. "Come in."

He held the door to his office for her, then closed it behind her.

He didn't move away from her. He stood close enough to touch her, one hand on the doorknob, the other still tucked into his pocket.

The memory of their near-kiss on the courthouse lawn distracted her into making a small movement, averting her eyes, turning her head just a fraction of an inch.

It was enough to break the tension. Cord walked across the room, then turned and faced her, leaning against the edge of his desk. "What is it?" he asked.

"My apprentice carpenter—Andy Gerhardt—has been arrested," she said without moving away from the door.

"Why?"

"He was at the job site here on Chestnut Street."

Cord pushed himself up from the desk. His face betrayed no reaction, but his momentary silence grated in her ears. "And just what was he doing there?" His tone was neutral, but Arianna didn't miss the disapproval.

"The district attorney questioned my crew. He told them someone had planned an 'accident' for the building. A fire."

Cord muttered a word she didn't catch, but she had no doubt it was succinct and graphic.

She felt a hot flush creep up from her collar, tinged with a sharp regret for her impulse to come to him with this. He was working without a fee, as a favor to Charlie, on a job she'd never intended to be this complicated or emotionally draining.

She should have gone to a different lawyer. It hadn't occurred to her, though. She wasn't used to having to ask for legal favors on behalf of her employees, to being the cause of police procedures and wrong-side-of-the-law mistakes and complicated terms of what was owed and what was not.

"If you'll just tell me what's needed," she said, with dignity, "I'll arrange to bail him out. You don't have to go there yourself. And of course I'll pay whatever fee you charge for the consultation."

The look he gave her expressed clear disbelief, but he said only a restrained, "I'll take care of it."

"That's not necessary. I'm responsible."

"No, you're not."

"But I'm the one who—"

"You didn't violate the order. Gerhardt knew he wasn't supposed to be there."

"But the D.A. said—"

"Oslund is an overambitious son of a bitch who uses a lot of unsavory police procedures to pressure potential witnesses."

Surprised at both his tone of voice and the harsh pronouncement, Ari broke off, silent.

He ran a hand through his hair, then spun around to face the big window framing a view of high-rise office buildings and the smaller, ornately Victorian city hall of an older Worcester.

Ari's wary gaze moved from the view back to Cord's tense shoulders and steel-straight back. "You think the district attorney . . . *made up* the evidence?"

"I don't know. Maybe. Maybe not. Maybe the same party that put those forged invoices into your desk went back to the job."

Her breath caught. "To burn it?"

"Your apprentice shouldn't have been at that job," he said, his back still to her, his voice controlled again.

"But he just—"

Cord turned around toward her. "Just *what?*"

The barked question took her aback. She swallowed. "I can't leave this up to you. It's my responsibility. I have my checkbook, and—"

He swore, low and indecipherable, but with enough anger to stop her midsentence. "Your apprentice is at best a damn fool and at worst criminally involved, Arianna. Either way, you are *not* responsible for his actions, and you are sure as hell not going to bail him out."

She blinked, shocked at the rough words.

"I'll take care of Gerhardt," Cord said with enough edge to cut through her bafflement. "If you insist on coming with me, I'll allow that, but you'll stay out of the police station and out of the case and your name won't appear on any bail bond that gets signed. Is that clear?"

Her cheeks grew hot as she took in his meaning. She was being naive. Acting like her father, on an impulse of righteous outrage that ignored the finer points of manipulating the system. That would make her look criminally involved.

She straightened her spine and clenched her jaw against the resentment of injustice that wanted to answer him. "Yes," she said, making her voice level and her gaze steady. "It's quite clear."

"Ari—"

She caught no more than a flicker of apology, then he killed whatever words he'd intended. "We can take my car."

She nodded. "All right."

She didn't wait for him to open the door for her. With hard-fought dignity she preceded him out of the office and down to the street, but an ache in her chest had replaced the quick flare of anger she'd felt in his office.

She knew he wouldn't apologize to her. He couldn't. Just as he couldn't chance touching her. He wouldn't risk his case and his client on anything so nebulous as an emotional impulse. His world didn't consider emotion a valid reason for action. Not emotion. Not family. Not outrage that the simple truth wasn't good enough. Not trust.

It was a short, silent drive to the police station. Cord parked on the street, fed a quarter into the meter, then leaned in the open door of the Mercedes and held out a handful of change.

"I shouldn't be long, but if the meter runs out, feed it, all right?"

"All right."

He hesitated for a moment, his hands still gripping the edge of the roof, as if he would say something more, then he pushed away and slammed the door.

Arianna watched him cross the street and walk into the gray stone fortress that was the police station. Then she stared straight ahead at the walnut paneling of the dashboard, seeing nothing.

When the weight of her thoughts closed in unbearably, she reached for the door handle and got out of the car.

She realized her mistake on the first breath of cold city air.

Oslund, the district attorney, was standing on the opposite side of the car.

"Good afternoon, Ms. Rossini."

Ari said nothing.

"Where's your lawyer?" he asked her. "Bailing out your coworker? You are keeping Prescott busy, aren't you?"

She stopped herself from answering. The chill of cold air seeped into the pit of her stomach. What she saw in Oslund's eyes was ice.

"Why don't we get in?" he asked casually, ignoring the outrage in her reaction.

The door was unlocked, the window open. She couldn't stop him. He eased his bulky figure into the driver's side of the Mercedes, sitting in Cord's place, in Cord's car, as if the action were an everyday occurrence. Ari fought a thread of panic, wondering what he wanted.

Don't react, she warned herself.

"I was quite surprised at your not-guilty plea this morning," he said. "When Prescott bailed you out, he implied you wouldn't be contesting this case. I guess you've changed his mind."

The words were bland, but the implications behind them carried menace.

A flicker of anger replaced her panic. She got into the front seat beside him. "I'm not guilty, Mr. Oslund."

"So, it seems, you've convinced your lawyer."

She didn't contradict him, though the words jammed her throat.

"This would be much easier on both of you, you know, if you had entered a guilty plea."

She started to answer him, then stopped herself before she spoke.

His eyes narrowed. "No dealing, no argument, no controversy, with a nolo plea. You know, you may have your lawyer convinced, Ms. Rossini, but a judge and a jury are a different thing. It is not a given that a woman can get away with fraud and embezzlement. No matter how good looking she is."

Her throat was dry. "I'm not—"

"And it would be such a pity to bring your father into this case, wouldn't it?"

The driver's side door was yanked open with

enough force to shake the Mercedes on its tires. "Get out," Cord said from the sidewalk. The low command was uttered with a controlled fury that Arianna read in the taut lines of his face and the set of his jaw.

Oslund stared at him, unmoving. "Your client invited me in."

Arianna didn't bother to dispute the comment. She pushed open her door and got out of the car, an instinctual act to diffuse the tension, and a reaction of blind aversion to the man sitting beside her in Cord's seat.

"Get out," Cord said again to Oslund.

Taking his time, the D.A. obeyed.

"Sooner or later she'll have to talk to me, Prescott." Oslund ignored Ari as she circled the car to stand beside Cord.

"What did this discussion involve?" Cord asked, his jaw still clenched.

The D.A. turned to her and smiled, his eyes cold. "It involved Arianna's . . . best interest, I guess you'd say."

"Are you threatening my client, Oslund?"

"Oh, no." He smiled at Ari again. "Give my regards to your father."

Ari's heart thudded in her chest. She didn't trust her voice.

As if he enjoyed her panic, Oslund stepped closer. "Keep it in mind, sweetheart," he said, touching her face with one finger.

Cord's reaction was so explosive, she couldn't

take in the order of events. His fist connected with Oslund's jaw hard enough to make a sickening *smack* in the bright air. Oslund's head snapped back, his body rammed into the side of the Mercedes, and Cord's briefcase full of papers scattered across the pavement.

"Cord—no!" She stepped in front of him, her hands flat on his chest, pushing him away. He was already backing off, though, letting Oslund heft himself on his elbows on the back of the car.

He stayed there for a moment, unmoving except for the small tic of fury in his cheek and the harsh breathing of poisonous anger. Then he straightened, pressed his palm against his jaw, and examined his fingers, as if checking for blood. "You son of a bitch. What makes you think you can get away with this?"

Cord said nothing.

"You got your job from your old man, Prescott. Everybody knows it. But you don't remember everything he taught you, do you? You're not quite as smart as your partner. You just did something very stupid."

The air was so charged with tension, it could have been visible. A car slowed on the street. Someone coming out of the police station hesitated, staring at them, reading the aftershock like a news headline.

One glance at Cord's face told her he took Oslund's accusation as truth. His jaw was clamped shut, his posture tense. She didn't move, afraid of doing anything that would breach the control he so valued.

Oslund yanked his suit jacket back into place on his shoulders and took a step away from the car. Cord's shift of weight was a small, conscious movement that put him slightly in front of her, the body language so subtle, it seemed almost casual. But his words, though deceptively soft, left no doubt of his intent. "If you want to talk to Ms. Rossini, you can do it through me," he said with unnatural calm.

Oslund stared at him a moment longer, then turned on his heel and walked toward the police station, his spine stiff and his footsteps pounding the pavement with emphasis.

Ari stood where she was, utterly still, as if she couldn't imagine what ordinary human actions could follow such an encounter.

Cord glanced at her, caught her gaze with his own, and smiled, a small movement that dispelled some of the tension. "Are you all right, Ms. Rossini?" he asked mildly, with a hint of humor, as if he could dismiss the violence of the last few minutes by an act of will.

She nodded.

"You don't look it," he said.

"Neither do you."

"It's hard work, making the right career moves sometimes."

He made her smile, though it was shaky. "What can he do to get even?"

Cord studied her, then apparently realized she wouldn't settle for evasive answers. "He can refuse to play ball on your case, Ari. But that's not in his best interest. He's been getting his hands dirty on this. He knows I could make him look like he's been playing in the mud. I'd take pleasure in it, as a matter of fact."

There was a chill in his voice that skipped all the way down her spine. When he looked at her again, his eyes were hard. "What did he say to you?"

"He wanted me to plead nolo."

Cord swore.

"What do you mean—he's been playing in the mud?"

He slanted her a glance. "He has a personal gripe against your family, Ari. He had money invested in the company your father was working for when he was indicted. Later on, when the company went under, he lost his investment."

"But—he blames my father for that? And me?"

"Let's just say he's pushing a little too hard for a guilty plea. And if he could get one without even going to trial, it would look awfully good on his record."

"Oh." It was a small sound. "It would probably look better on your record, too, wouldn't it? If you didn't get involved."

"Oslund isn't worried about my record, Ari, except for the times I've won against him. Don't let him get to you. That's what you have lawyers for. To protect you against those kind of low-life tactics."

But who would protect the lawyer? Guilt cut a swathe through her uneven emotions. Oslund had already gotten to Cord through her. Enough to make him lose control, something she knew he'd have to pay for, one way or another.

"What will happen now?" she asked.

His expression was composed again, reassuring, lawyerlike. "Nothing much. I'll handle Oslund. I know him pretty well. He'll deal if he thinks it's his own tail on the line."

"I don't want you to have to do that," she said. "To . . . appease him."

"Don't look so worried, Ms. Rossini. I learned young how to sleep with the enemy. It's not something you forget, if you're a good lawyer."

"I can't imagine you'd be any good at it."

"You might be surprised."

The last sentence held too much irony, too many layers of disillusionment. It hurt to hear it. Ari looked away from him, her arms crossed in front of her. "Is Andy all right?" she asked finally.

"Yes. I gave him cab fare back to his car."

"Thank you."

"For what it's worth, he said he didn't find any crossed wires."

She looked back at him. "For what it's worth?"

"I can't use it in court. He wasn't supposed to

be there. But it will provide a little leverage against Oslund."

Leverage. Deals. Sleeping with the enemy. She swallowed hard. "Oh. I see."

Cord let it go. He bent to sweep up his scattered papers, snapped the briefcase closed, and straightened with it in his hand, his face set. "Look," he said without emotion, "take the Mercedes back to your truck. You can leave it in front of the office."

"Why? Where are you going?"

"There's a bar not far from here, where the legal crowd hangs out. I'm betting Oslund's there getting a drink. I'll catch up with him."

"I'll go with you."

Cord stared at her a long moment. "You're not going with me, Ari."

"Why not?"

"Because," he said deliberately, "you're going to distance yourself from any complications in this case. Because you're not going to bring anyone's attention to the fact that you were here when I bailed Andy out."

"But Oslund already knows—"

"No argument, Ari."

The words stopped her cold, not so much the meaning as the cynicism that shaded them.

"Because that's the way the game is played?" Her own voice sounded brittle, like a thin skim of ice over spring thaw.

He took his time before he answered her,

thinking about it. "No," he said finally. "Because I promised Pop I'd keep you out of jail."

The unexpected words loosed a core of emotion that filled Ari's chest and pressed at her throat. As if a barrier had been peeled away, she was aware, with acute sensitivity, of the small reactions that betrayed the emotions Cord fought so hard to cover with professional distance—the tension in his shoulders, the carefully unclenched fists, the straight posture as he pulled his keys out of his pocket and held them out to her.

She glanced down at the dangling keys, but made no move to take them. "You promised me something too," she said, raising her eyes to his. "You promised me you'd keep Pop out of this. You said we'd be working together."

It hadn't been a promise. She knew that, and she knew he wanted to tell her that. She could read it in the way his mouth quirked, and by the glint of frustration in his eyes.

He didn't say it, though. Silence spun out between them, weighted with emotions still unsorted, confusing, disturbing. It occurred to her, bit by bit, that something had changed between them. Something more fragile than the taut, braided cord of desire she'd felt outside the courthouse, but deeper, closer to the bone, more momentous in its consequences.

He closed his fingers around the keys, slowly, and pulled his hand back. He shook his head, a gesture of bafflement rather than denial, and gave her a slow smile that made her pulse skip.

"All right, Arianna Rossini," he said. "We'll work as a team. It'll just be you and me."

She thought she should smile back at the irony, but the message underneath it was too unsettling. *Just you and me.*

She knew that he was offering her something she'd asked him for, outside the courthouse, on the lawn. In taking it, she'd owe him something back, something that had nothing to do with money or obligation or the law. Something more costly and more valuable than any of those. She felt a surge of longing, with a shaft of fear inside it. What was she doing?

"I'll go with you, then," she said.

He nodded. Then, leaning close enough to her so that she could smell the mixed scents of aftershave, clean wool gabardine, and cotton, but without touching her anywhere, he opened the door of the car and let her in.

SIX

Eddie's Grille was warm, dimly lit, and full of lawyers. Oslund wasn't among them, Cord decided as soon as he walked in. The buzz of conversation was subdued and civilized, punctuated now and then by the click of pool balls from the single table in the billiards room behind the bar. There was no gossip-network reaction as they made their way into the room, toward the long, scrubbed pine bar that flanked a stone fireplace.

"Oslund's not here," Cord said, glancing around the room just to be sure.

He could sense Ari's tension, her discomfort with the crowd that filled the bar. "Come on. We don't have to stay here."

She nodded, accepting his decision. Touching her arm as they turned back toward the door, he had to check the urge to run his palm along her back, to put his arm around her shoulders.

Protect her from the world.

The urge shocked him more than the fact that half an hour earlier he'd driven his fist into the side of the district attorney's face.

In one day he seemed to have broken every rule he'd ever set for himself. Professional distance. Self-interest. Objectivity. The dictates of the law.

"Cord!"

From the arched doorway of the grille's back room, a dark-haired woman in a blue silk suit waved a pool cue and grinned at Cord. She made her way toward them through the tables while her pool partner straightened up from his shot and watched her defection, looking resigned.

"Cord! How are you?"

"I'm fine, Elaine," he said, turning to face her, hiding his internal protest at the intrusion. "Arianna Rossini, Elaine Andress. Elaine's a reporter for the *Telegram*."

Elaine gave Ari a generous smile, dropped an oversize camera case on the bar, and leaned an elbow beside it. "How do you do? So—where has Cord been keeping himself?"

"The usual story," Cord said. "Work."

"Oh, well. We all do *that*." She hooked the toe of her shoe around a stool and pulled it toward her. She perched on it, using her pool cue as a makeshift crutch, then lifted the cue to wave at the bartender at the other end of the bar.

Elaine caught Ari's expression and lowered the

pool cue, laughing. "I know. This thing can be dangerous. But then, Cord taught me to play." She raised her eyebrows in mock conspiracy. "The pool cue as a weapon. Get him to show you sometime. He's incredible. He can run the table whenever he likes. I'll buy," she announced to the bartender. "How about it, Cord? Drinks all around?"

He smiled slightly. "No thanks, Elaine. We're on our way out."

Elaine made a face. "Just for me then," she told the bartender, then grinned at Ari. "Do you and Cord work together?"

Ari hesitated. "No. I'm—"

"She's a family friend of my partner's," Cord broke in.

Elaine turned toward him. "Charlie? Really? He's such a sweetheart. Now, Charlie knows how to be discreet, too, but he doesn't just disappear from view when he has a new . . . interest."

"I'll tell him you said so."

"Please do." She laughed. "If you see him before I do." She smiled brightly from Cord to Ari, managing to imply that she and Charlie had a relationship that had been hitherto unannounced. He was supposed to ask about it, Cord surmised, if only to express a polite degree of jealousy. He let it pass, though, unwilling to prolong the conversation by investigating Elaine's current status with his law partner.

"Well," Elaine said. "I suppose they can send

my drink over to the billiards room, can't they?" She rose from the stool with exuberant energy and wagged two fingers at them in parting, then made her way back to her pool partner, her cue tucked under her arm like a baton, breezy nonchalance unfazed.

It was a quality, Cord thought, that he had once found attractive in her. Perhaps he still would, if he saw her in a different place, a different time. But his appreciation for facile charm had paled in the past few days, replaced by an awakened awareness of some qualities that outshone it.

He touched Ari's shoulder again, then followed her out of the bar to the sidewalk, his eyes on the straight, supple line of her back, his thoughts on the direct, unswerving way she confronted the truth, his emotions caught on the vulnerability of her position.

She stopped at the curb, waiting for him to come up beside her to walk to his car. "Thank you," she said, "for not mentioning that I'm a client. And for not staying. I know I said I could handle the fallout from all this, but I guess I'm not as . . . prepared as I thought I was."

"It wasn't any sacrifice for me to leave. I didn't want to talk to Elaine. When I need something from the press, I can call her. Not now."

Ari appeared startled. "You mean she was looking for information?"

"Elaine's always looking for information. I give it to her sometimes. She's . . . a friend."

In the street beside them a car passed. A reflection of the late-afternoon sunlight slanted off the windshield, flickering across her face. "Yes. I see," she said with that dignity that caught at his conscience.

"Euphemisms aren't part of your vocabulary, are they?" he murmured. "She was a lover," he added when Ari glanced at him. "It's been over for a while."

"You don't have to explain to me."

"I know."

They walked on in silence, the only sound was their matched footsteps on the pavement.

She looked at him again. "I was raised to think that was important. Explaining. Telling the truth. That if you just told the truth, everything would come out right in the end."

"It's not a bad way to be raised, Ari," he said gently.

She nodded. "It's not an easy habit to break, either. I keep thinking if I just explain, then everything will be all right."

"You don't counter threats and intimidation by trying to explain yourself. It doesn't work."

He could sense her studying him, seeing more than he'd meant to reveal. She said, staring at the side of his face, "Did you learn that from your father?"

He considered brushing her off, or simply not answering, but he made the mistake of meeting her eyes and reading that innate honesty she seemed to wear like she wore her perfume. It must have been catching. "Yeah. Early on."

"How do you counter threats, then?"

". . . By being a lawyer."

They'd reached the corner, a small square of brick sidewalk partly screened from the street by a budding maple tree. She stopped there, facing him, and he watched a sheen of moisture brighten her eyes.

"Does it work?" she asked.

His voice thickened. "It works well enough, Ari. You don't have to feel anything about it."

A smile flickered across her mouth, then was gone. "That's a lawyer's way of phrasing it, isn't it? I don't have to feel anything. It's not required. As if it's a chore I can be released from."

He shut his eyes for a moment. "That's what I am. A lawyer."

"You keep saying that. Next you're going to tell me what you want doesn't matter, because you're a lawyer. You're not required to want anything."

What he wanted was to touch her. To trace the curve of her mouth and the oval of her face, and to watch a new kind of tension come into the transparent expressions of her face. Inside his pants' pockets, Cord curled his fingers into his palms.

She put her hand on his sleeve, lightly, with no suggestiveness, a touch that was meant as a substitute for words, but it went through him like wild-fire.

Slowly, deliberately, he turned fully toward her, studying her with a stillness that could almost have been objective detachment.

It wasn't.

The late-afternoon sunlight, filtered by the delicate, new-formed foliage behind her, touched the side of her face and reflected ephemeral glints of light in the dark brown of her eyes and the pale gold of her lashes. In the building behind them, a fan vibrated into the dusk, like a faint afterimage of the bar they'd just left, emphasizing the privacy of the deserted street corner, humming with the provocative knowledge that there was no one around to see them.

"You're not like any client I've ever had, Arianna Rossini."

"How am I different?"

"I can't begin to tell you all the ways." He pulled one hand out of his pocket, circled her wrist where she touched his arm, then brought her hand up between them. He pressed his thumb against the hollow of her wrist, where her heartbeat pulsed, then cupped her fingers, brushing his thumb along the small mark where she'd cut herself in her father's kitchen.

She smiled, a slight sketch of expression that somehow increased the sudden intimacy between them. "You've just never met a woman who had calluses, maybe."

"Oh, yes. I've met lots of them. The difference is that you have them only on your hands."

Her breath caught, and in the fading light the swift understanding in her eyes coursed through him like the life surge of sap in a spring tree.

"I never hit anybody before in my life. But I'd do it again, you know that? I wish to God I'd hit him harder. I wish I could knock his underhanded tactics and his two-bit gangster mind-set into next week."

"I thought that was what you did."

He lifted his free hand to her face, brushing her cheek as if the touch could heal his bruised knuckles, then he ran his thumb along the outline of her lower lip, barely touching her.

"Maybe it is," he said. "Maybe what I want now is the spoils of battle."

She moved, finally, capturing his wrist in her hand, finding his pulse. "I know," she whispered.

"If you knew what I wanted, lady, you'd tell me to go to hell and take my Helen of Troy fantasies with me."

"I don't think so. I think it would take more than that to shock me."

His eyes darkened, studying her face. Then he gathered her hand against his chest, pulling her a step closer, tipping her face up toward his with a hand under her chin.

"How much more?" he asked, his voice gruff. "The fact that it doesn't seem to matter to me that you're a client?"

"No . . ."

"How about the fact that I don't give a damn right now about lawyers' ethics? Or the reputation of my law firm. Or anything else except this?" With one arm he circled her back and dragged her forcefully against him, hip to hip, thigh to thigh.

His body responded to the contact, growing hard, aroused, taut with the tension of needed release.

She pressed one hand to his hip, her body pliant against his, refusing to fight him. "I know what you care about, Cord," she whispered. "I've had a lot of practice with the truth. Sometimes it's not what it should be. But what have I done that makes you think I can't handle it?"

It was another question that cut straight through to the core and stripped away all possibility of a facile answer. What the hell had she ever done to make him think she wasn't strong enough to handle the truth?

Nothing. She knew what he was. She knew how little of his soul he had left to offer. They both knew it. Kissing her wouldn't change that.

Kissing her wouldn't change anything.

He didn't go any further with that logic. He didn't have to. He was too good a lawyer to know it wouldn't hold up in court for fifteen seconds. But he wanted her too badly to listen to logic.

Still holding her hips flush against him, he lowered his head the last inch and touched her lips with slow, exquisite care, a care that was sharply at odds with the rough way he held her. He fit their mouths together with deliberate and consummate intent, sealing the sensitive contact as though to end any possibility of pretending this intimacy could not happen.

He moved his head, parting her lips, seeking the deeper intimacy of open mouths and silken penetration, as Ari's eyes slid closed and her thoughts scattered like breaking glass.

His hands cupped her backside, pulling her closer, and she yielded to them, arching her back, opening her mouth.

The reasons he'd given her for keeping distance from him receded from her mind, spinning backward, silenced by the drumming of her heart, the melting weakness in her body, the heart-tripping shock of her tongue against his.

She had no defenses against that kind of shock, that kind of heat, that kind of sudden, all-consuming desire. She gave herself to the rough, velvet demands of his tongue, his hands, his body with a soft, wordless sound of need that spoke a language deeper than words. Shaping his back with her hands, chasing the movements of his tongue with her own, she shared a searching intimacy that raced beyond thought or inhibition until the heat of it plunged into the deepest part of her body and turned it to liquid fire.

With a muffled groan Cord broke off the kiss. He dragged her more tightly against him as he dropped his head back and swallowed convulsively.

Their breathing was harsh, rushed, forced into an unnatural constraint of control after an act that had plummeted them over the edge in one explosive moment.

Slowly, with careful discipline, he moved away from her, pulling back, though he still held her lightly around the hips.

He shut his eyes, his expression strained. "Ari . . ."

"It's all right." She forced the tight, pinched words from her throat as if they could alleviate her own desire that had flared to life like a struck match, and the nerve-grazing frustration of its denial. Even refusing to look at him, she could feel his gaze, carrying heat the way his hand had, his mouth, his body.

"I don't think so," he said, the words faintly ironic, carrying no more conviction or control than hers.

Working at it, she raised her chin and made herself look at him. He looked, she realized, shaken—baffled, as if he'd just been told something he couldn't believe. The gray eyes were intense and searching, the mouth she'd just kissed taut, turned down at the corners, the expression marked with shock.

"I don't care about your 'professional ethics,' you know," she said. "That doesn't mean anything to me. I wasn't brought up to care about those kinds of rules."

"I know you weren't. That's *my* job. The rules. The system." His voice was still raw, rough edged with the effort of control.

"Is *everything* your job?" she snapped rebelliously.

He didn't answer her. She dropped her eyes and breathed out a silent resignation to the answer she knew he would give her.

She needed his professional expertise, his detachment, his cold manipulation of the system. She needed him to keep her out of jail.

But she needed something else from him too. His touch. His kiss. The sensuality that sang between them now, and more than that, she needed his trust, his affection, his friendship.

Maybe even his love. Maybe more than he could give.

She squeezed her eyes shut, holding back the tears that threatened. She was the one who had told him she could handle the truth.

He let her go, stepping back from her and turning away. He hooked a hand on the nape of his neck and tipped his head forward to rub out the knots, then looked up again, back toward the bar they'd just left.

Something in the set of his shoulders, the way he went still, caught her attention, jolting her out of her conflicted, ambivalent needs. She turned her head to follow his line of sight.

District Attorney Oslund was getting out of a car at the end of the block. He walked into the bar by himself, burly shoulders hunched as he yanked open the door and let himself in.

She felt a chill that cut through the still-heated atmosphere like a sliver of ice. The realization of why they'd come there dragged her back, plunging her down into that chill.

Cord's world, the one he'd just claimed he no longer cared about, pushed itself into her consciousness, shouldering aside her desperate wish that reality could be different from what it was.

Cord dropped his hand, then turned to look at her. "You don't have to go back in, Ari. I can take you home first."

"No."

"Ari . . ."

She didn't answer. The silence was heavy with the words not spoken, weighted with unresolved emotion and still-needful desire.

Another car passed them and turned the corner, then Cord let out a long breath. "If that arrogant son of a bitch touches you again, I'll put a fist into the other side of his face." Without giving her so much as the chance to take in the comment, he turned and walked her back to Eddie's Grille.

Inside, Oslund was seated at the bar, flanked by empty stools, as if his mood was sending out emanations that repelled casual drinkers. Cord crossed the room and leaned against the bar beside him. He waited, his presence ominous, until Oslund glanced up, forced to acknowledge him. "Can I do something for you?" the D.A. said finally. "Or is this just a fortunate coincidence?"

Cord ignored the sarcasm. "We have some unfinished business, Oslund. I thought it would be a good idea to take care of it before it gets out of hand."

Oslund's lip curled, but he made a grudging gesture with one hand. "Sit down."

Cord gestured for Ari to take the stool. Reluctance to sit beside Oslund lodged in her chest like something she'd swallowed whole, but she made herself ignore it. Oslund gave her a long, insolent look, gauging her reaction. Behind her she could feel Cord's mood harden, the tension tighten another notch, but he didn't move, didn't speak.

Oslund broke the impasse first. "You going to give me some good reason I shouldn't bring you up on assault charges, Prescott?"

"No," Cord said, his voice low and controlled, vibrant with dangerous undercurrents.

The district attorney took a leisurely sip of his drink. "Playing it straight?" he asked. "You changing your style, Prescott?"

Cord waited a long moment before speaking. "Andy Gerhardt is no criminal, Oslund. He was duped. You didn't find any crossed wires in that renovation."

"The evidence," Oslund said, drawling the words, "is open to interpretation."

"What evidence?"

There was a silence.

"What was your source, Oslund?"

Caught in his slip of revealing more than he'd intended, Oslund flushed darkly, shooting Cord a venomous look. "Maybe I didn't have a source."

"Then that makes it coercion, doesn't it?" Cord said coolly. "You know it. I know it."

"You can't prove it in court."

"Do you want it brought up?" Cord leaned a little closer. "You want to watch me bring it up and introduce evidence against it?"

"That's standard police tactics, Prescott. An interpretation of the evidence. If your client fell for the bait, it's your loss."

"*My* client didn't fall for the bait."

The district attorney's cheek twitched in unconscious acknowledgment of another mistake.

"She has no reason to," Cord added deliberately. "My client is innocent."

Oslund banged his drink down on the bar hard enough to make the liquor splash over the rim. In spite of herself, Ari jumped, a reaction to the biting anger simmering beneath Oslund's thin facade. He stared at her, his hand clenched around the glass, before he looked back at Cord. "Since when?"

Ari's eyes flicked to Cord. Her heart was hammering in her throat, and a coil of fear tightened in her chest.

Pushed beyond shrewdness by Cord's lack of

reaction, Oslund snatched up the drink again and glared directly at Ari. "We all know your history, Ms. Rossini. You had plenty of chance to learn the trade, didn't you? Like father, like daughter. It's no secret."

For Ari, the surroundings of the bar went an unnatural shade of gray. She felt a burgeoning explosion of emotion she couldn't identify, but before any of it found expression, Cord's hand clamped down on her shoulder, hard, solid, shocking her into looking at him. His face was impassive, giving nothing away to the man beside them. His grip on her shoulder wasn't intimate, but the possessive, protective message of the gesture was too clear to be misinterpreted.

Oslund's eyes narrowed as he stared at Cord's hand, then he shifted his gaze to Ari's face. She felt the tenor of his thoughts as if he'd stated them aloud.

"My client's family history is inadmissible in court, Oslund," Cord said. "You bring it up and I just might find a way to trot out your personal vendetta in this case. Your investment in Wilson Graphics. I don't think that would serve your purposes."

"What the hell do you want, Prescott? A trial? Is that what you're telling me?"

Cord let the question lie, but his grip on Ari's shoulder relaxed. "You play pool?" he asked the older man.

Unexpected and seemingly unconnected, the

casual suggestion defused the explosive pitch of Oslund's reaction. The man blinked, frowned, and Ari glanced at Cord in surprise.

"You break," Cord said to Oslund. "Your choice of game."

It followed no rules of legal interchange for Cord to offer, and it made no objective sense for the district attorney to agree to the game. But Cord's challenge had been gauged to a precise calculation, and, watching Oslund, Ari realized just how subtle that calculation had been.

Oslund would take the challenge.

The big man tossed back the last of his drink, pulled his suit jacket straight, and stood up.

Apprehensive, on edge in response to the alien currents she could sense but not interpret, Ari followed the two men toward the billiards room. Elaine and her partner were leaning against the table, pool cues beside them, the table empty.

"Cord," Elaine said, glancing toward them. "I thought you'd left. Are you looking for the table?"

"Yes. If you're through with it."

"Oh, we are." Elaine's curious, amused gaze flicked toward the D.A. "Frank. I didn't know you'd come in."

"And I didn't know you were here," Oslund told her.

She smiled. "Catch you later, Frank. Cord. Ari."

With admirable grace she swept herself, her drink, and her escort out of the billiards room, oblivious to Cord's frown and Ari's uncomprehending shake of her head.

When Ari looked back again, Oslund was staring at her. He gave her a shrewd, assessing smile. "Are you joining this game, Ms. Rossini?" The polite title of address was drawled enough to make it an insult.

Ari ignored the tone and repressed her shudder of dislike. "No. I'll bring drinks, though, if you'd like."

"Whiskey and soda," Oslund said.

She glanced toward Cord.

"Yes, coffee. Thanks," he told her.

The clatter of the pool balls followed her as she turned toward the bar, as though Oslund couldn't wait to start the game.

When she came back with the drinks, Oslund's smile had turned feral. She didn't play the game, but it didn't take a pool shark to see that Oslund was winning, making his shots, gloating that Cord had missed his opening shot.

Oslund took the drink she gave him without thanking her. "I don't suppose, Ms. Rossini," he said, "that you've heard your lawyer's nickname among the legal community?"

She didn't answer him, but he went on just as if she had.

"Ace," Oslund said, slanting her a glance as he leaned over the table. He pulled the pool cue back, stroked it, and his ball thumped into the pocket. Pleased, smug, Oslund straightened and looked at her. "His nickname is Ace. Because he so seldom loses. Not even the *pro bono* cases."

Like hers. With effort, she kept herself from showing any reaction.

"The last pro bono case he took was that Mc-Cormack kid indicted for armed robbery. The convenience store. You remember that case?"

She couldn't bring herself not to answer. She shook her head.

"Couple years ago. We thought we had him in the bag. But your lawyer—"

Oslund broke off midsentence to take another shot. He missed it. With a faint what-the-hell sneer he straightened and faced Ari. "Your lawyer got him off. Scot-free. Not guilty. Thing is . . ."

He paused for effect, enjoying the imminent point of his story, deriving sick pleasure from her anticipated reaction. That much she knew. Cord was standing at the other end of the table, his pool cue loosely gripped in one hand, his face absolutely devoid of expression. Still, Ari could sense that under the smooth facade, his emotions were strung taut at this antagonistic interchange she didn't yet understand.

". . . Thing is," Oslund went on, "the kid pulled the same kind of job three months later. Mom-and-pop convenience store. This time, he shot the owners." Oslund picked up his drink, sipped it, then held it up toward Ari in a mock salute. "You probably remember that one, don't you? The Minhs? She died."

Stricken by the sudden memory, her outrage then at the crime, the unexpected fact of Cord's part in it, Ari couldn't manage even a nod. Oslund's satisfied smile showed her what her face must reveal. A surge of anger at him rose into her throat, hot and raw. Cord would have taken responsibility for that acquittal, she knew. He would have blamed himself for the woman's death. And Oslund was using that knowledge to get back at him for the wounds to Oslund's ego that he couldn't salve with legitimate retaliation.

Cord's slow, even, seemingly casual comment broke into the silence. "It's not a perfect system, Oslund. We all work in it." He moved around the table.

The *smack* of the cue ball against its target, too hard, sent the shot careening off the side, scattering balls across the table.

"Bad shot, Prescott," Oslund said with vicious pleasure. "But then, we all know you're sometimes capable of a bad call. Especially Mrs. Minh, huh?" His smile slid from Cord to Ari. "Even Ace Prescott doesn't get lucky all the time."

She sought out Cord's gaze as if it could give her a lifeline against Oslund's insinuations. He looked back at her, steady, competent. He didn't bother to look at the table again until Oslund had conceded his turn.

When Cord leaned over the green felt, gauging angles and direction, he was standing opposite her, lining up a shot directly in her sight. He studied it, hesitated, and moved the angle of the cue.

A craftsman herself, she recognized manual skill in someone else. She recognized it now. Cord was missing his shots on purpose.

Cocky and increasingly arrogant, Oslund took his turn with a careless shrug and a smirk that didn't attempt to hide his enjoyment of Cord's seemingly inevitable defeat.

"So, Prescott," Oslund drawled. "You think you can prove your client is *innocent*? You want to take this case to trial?"

Cord gave her not a glance. She gripped the edge of the pool table and made a strangled sound in the back of her throat, but, caught up in their contest, neither man heard it.

Cord leaned over the table and took his shot. The cue ball smacked against its target and recoiled back toward another, and two balls clattered unerringly into the pockets. Cord took his next shot, and the next, working with cold, efficient skill that had Oslund gaping in bafflement and growing realization, his face flushed and angry.

"That's right, Oslund," Cord said. "I think you've got the message." He hit another shot, circled the table, leaned over it, sank the next ball, then straightened and stared across the table at the district attorney. "You want a court fight, Oslund, you've got it. And I'll take on your case and run it off the table."

Oslund's succinct, crude epithet exploded through the small room. Around the tables in the main part of the restaurant, astonished faces turned toward them, conversations flagging.

Beyond caring about the potential audience for this duel, the district attorney repeated his curse, staring at Cord.

There was one shot left on the table. One move left in the game. Cord took in the configuration, flicked a glance toward Oslund, then set his cue down on the green felt, declining to make that last move. "See you in court, Oslund," he said quietly, then with a touch at Arianna's back, guided her through the murmuring crowd to the street outside.

SEVEN

They didn't speak, walking in silence out of the bar and past the corner where he'd kissed her, to his car. She slammed the passenger door shut after her and twined her hands together in her lap tightly enough to whiten the knuckles.

As he pulled away from the curb she looked at him and said curtly, "You had no right to do that."

The accusation went through him the way none of Oslund's vicious insults had.

"Listen, Arianna. That's not something I would normally do in front of a client, but it was just—"

"Whether I was there or not, you had no right to do that. To . . . challenge him to a trial. You know I don't want a trial. You had no right to say that!"

"It was a maneuver, Arianna. Not a trial date."

"But you said—"

"What I said is off the record. It doesn't count. It's not admissible in court."

Stunned, she stared at him.

Cord dragged in a breath, looking away. He couldn't deny it. He'd had no right to fan her anxieties by mentioning a trial. Trample on her ideals. Haul her against him and kiss her the way he had half an hour ago.

He glanced toward her again, taking in just a glimpse of her profile, her red-gold hair, tumbling over her tensely held shoulders, her hands closed into fists in her lap. His own fingers curled around the steering wheel, and he had to fight an urge that he recognized as an instinct to wrap her in his arms and reassure her.

Cord swore under his breath.

She was right. He was wrong.

And now he was the one floundering around wondering how in hell he was going to handle the truth.

Maybe what just happened in Eddie's will take care of the problem, his internal devil's advocate taunted.

Maybe it would. Maybe he'd given her a look at who he was that would kill any chance she'd want to keep on trusting him. She sure as hell didn't look like she was going to trust him now.

He muttered another curse. This one made it to his vocal cords and blistered the air with enough heat to justify a demand for an explanation.

She said nothing, though. He flipped on the turn signal, made the turn, and pulled the Mercedes into the reserved space behind his office building, in the lot behind the cordoned-off entrance to the structure she'd been hired to renovate. After he shut off the engine and pulled the key out of the ignition, his slowly released breath was audible.

He didn't trust himself to look at her. He was too close to reaching across the seat and pulling her sweet body against his and kissing her again. Kissing her long and hard and hot enough to make her forget Oslund and the damn pool game with the see-you-in-court ending, and the fact that if the district attorney had his way she'd end up in prison, serving a sentence she'd already lived through secondhand with her father.

He said instead, brusquely, "I want you to come in and take a look at Andy's deposition. It should be ready by now. With any luck it's on my desk."

"Andy's deposition? What can I tell you about that?"

"Whether it coincides with your understanding of the facts."

"You mean whether I think Andy is *lying?*"

She had trouble even getting the words out, as if the possibility wasn't thinkable. Cord felt his jaw clench. "Look. You authorized me to plea-bargain this. The only condition you put on me was to leave Pop out of it. That was the deal. The rest of this is done my way."

"I didn't authorize you to lie."

"What I told Oslund wasn't a lie."

"It wasn't the *truth*, either."

"You want the truth, Arianna? This is it: What I did back there is nothing more or less than what I've done a dozen times in the past couple of years in my dealings with Oslund or one of his staff. I'm a lawyer, lady. I make deals. That's what you asked me to do. You want truth and justice, you can authorize me to go after it in court. Otherwise, I plan to manipulate and maneuver and pressure anybody who's susceptible to it, because that's the only way I know to keep you from going to jail."

Her eyes widened at his harsh tone, then darkened with a guilt that reached straight into Cord's conscience. She caught her lower lip between her teeth. "I'm . . . sorry. I had no right to say that."

"Ari—for God's sake. Don't—"

She was watching him with the steady, straight gaze that had struck him all the way down into his gut the first time he'd seen her in the holding cell at the courthouse.

"Don't what?" she asked him.

Don't apologize. Don't look like you're seeing the man you want to see when you look across that seat. Don't trust me to do the right thing.

He didn't answer her.

"I'm asking you to do just that, aren't I?" she

said. "Manipulate the system. Make a deal." She sighed. "I have no right to put limits on how you do it. But I just didn't expect—"

Didn't expect her lawyer to assault the district attorney. Use her as bait in a pool game. Kiss her on a city street corner the way a man kisses a woman he intends to make love to.

"You didn't expect the tactics to be so rough," he said. "You didn't expect backdoor deals and intimidation and using what passes for truth as a weapon."

Her eyes widened again, this time with the recognition of profoundly dangerous ground. She wouldn't retreat from it.

"I know," she said softly. "I know what I'm asking you to do." Her throat worked. "I've known it for a long time. That's what Charlie wanted to do for my father, you see, and Pop wouldn't let him. He was so sure he'd be proved innocent. He had faith in the system. It was naive, I suppose. Stubborn. Stupid."

"No."

She made a faint, dismissive gesture with one hand, too reminiscent of the apology he hadn't wanted to hear.

"No," he said again. "Not stupid. Not that."

She went still for a moment, so unmoving that the change in color across her cheeks carried a message he could read.

"That boy," she said into the lengthening silence. "The one who killed the store owner. You didn't defend him the second time, did you?"

He didn't answer.

"Would you have the first time, if you believed he was guilty?"

"It was a job, Ari."

"A job? You didn't even get paid for it."

"Don't make out my motives to be too noble, lady."

"Why not?"

"Because one way or another, the spoils of battle is what I've always worked for."

Twin flames of emotion burned in her cheeks in acknowledgment of his reference to the kiss they'd shared on the street corner, but what he saw in response to his deliberately hard-edged answer was the rekindled flame of her anger.

"You haven't had much for your work, then, Mr. Prescott. One kiss surely isn't worth all the trouble of keeping me out of jail."

Don't count on it, babe. That was one hell of a kiss.

He turned away from her, leaned his head back on the seat, and closed his eyes. "You'd make one unbeatable prosecutor, Ms. Rossini. I'm glad you're not sitting across the courtroom from me."

She didn't answer. He turned his head to look at her. "You're right. I've gone to a lot more trouble for less."

She didn't say anything, but he saw her swallow hard.

"The McCormack kid . . . Charlie didn't

want me to take that case. The kid had done a couple of B and E's. Never got charged for them, but the cops knew it. When this armed robbery came up, they had him pegged for it. I thought he didn't do this one. The gun didn't fit his profile."

"Maybe he didn't."

Cord let out a huff of breath. "He did the next one. The Minhs. The woman who died. They had a daughter. High-school age. She witnessed it."

"That wasn't your fault, Cord. Oslund had no right to bring that up."

"I doubt Oslund gives a damn whose fault it was. He was making a point about my bad judgment. I had to show him he couldn't count on it again."

"By beating him on a pool table?"

"Pool table. Courtroom. It's just a different game, Ari. Just a matter of learning the shots."

"Learning to use the truth," she said reflectively, a little sadly. "For your own purposes. I understand."

Like one of the shots he'd just talked about, her quietly spoken comment reverberated through his gut as if she'd just run the table when he hadn't expected her to be a contender. She was right, he thought viciously. She had a pretty good grip on the truth herself, even when it hurt to face it.

Especially when it hurt to face it.

He shoved open the car door and got out. He wasn't sure, from the expression on her face, whether she'd come with him into the office. He wouldn't have blamed her if she didn't. She did, though.

Riding up in the elevator, she faced straight ahead, not looking at him, but close enough so that he could smell her perfume. It was one of the floral scents he'd seen in her bathroom the night he'd bandaged her finger, held her hand, and thought about the possibilities suggested by a glimpse of a white lace bedspread in a private room.

The receptionist was straightening up her desk when they walked in. She glanced at them, her eyes shifting from Cord to Ari and back again, curious and a bit speculative. She murmured a good evening. "The statement from Andy Gerhardt is on your desk, Mr. Prescott," she said crisply.

"Thank you," Cord told her.

"If you need more copies . . ."

"Not tonight, Ms. Walker. You can go on, if you were ready to leave. I'll lock up."

"Yes, then. Did I give you the message from Elaine Andress, Mr. Prescott?"

"I just saw her. Thank you."

Cord shut the door to his office behind them.

"Maybe you should take the message," Ari said. "She might have called since we left."

"No. She called earlier. The message was for Charlie, though, not for me. He's the one who gets calls from Elaine these days."

"Oh."

In the silence the sounds of the city street below seeped into the room. Ari walked over to the window, which was framed by ornate woodwork, discreetly curtained by semitransparent drapes, as if the chaotic outside world was allowed to intrude only so far into this opulent office. Turning, she saw one wall was lined with bookshelves, glass-fronted, fitted with locks. As if to keep the books from escaping, she thought wryly. Or the feelings.

For Cord, she knew, that dictate wasn't to be questioned. It was what he held as a belief. Ethics were framed to fit a profession instead of a life. Illusions were attacked like sins. Human emotions like trust and need were forbidden.

She knew better than to speak any of her thoughts. "Was this your father's office?"

"Yes. I moved into it after he died."

"Did you ever reconcile with him?"

"Not in the way you mean."

She looked at him, and he said, "Charlie took the place of my father. Substitute family. It works better than you might think."

She absorbed that, then smiled slightly. "You don't mind that he gets messages now from Elaine?"

"It's been a long time since I got personal messages from Elaine. Charlie . . . makes his own rules about his social life."

"I see."

Light from the window filtered into the room,

diffused and soft, tamed daylight. On the desk, in the middle of the blotter were two or three neatly typed sheets. Andy's statement. Ari stared at the papers for a moment, then Cord leaned toward the desk and picked them up. She watched him read through the statement, then he handed it to her.

The typed script was dry and succinct. Andy was an apprentice carpenter who had worked for Ms. Rossini for a year and a half. He had been warned by her to stay away from the job site after her arrest. He'd gone there because he wanted "to find out for himself" what he believed the district attorney had implied, and had been caught there by a uniformed officer. He had found nothing he interpreted as faulty wiring or a deliberate fire hazard, but he wasn't an electrician and possibly wouldn't recognize what he was looking for.

Ari handed the statement back without comment, then turned away toward the view of the city, her arms crossed in front of her.

"Do you think it was true what you said to the district attorney," she asked, "that there were no faulty wires? Do you think that was just a fabrication, something he made up to frighten my crew?"

"No. I think someone tipped him off to it. He wouldn't say who his source was, but I think he had a source."

She swallowed down protest in her throat and made her voice calm, though it sounded too husky in her own ears. "Why would someone do such a thing?"

"I can't think of any reason except to give Oslund another lever, more power. To put pressure on you. To make you feel trapped."

"To make me agree to a deal right away?"

". . . Maybe."

"But the police will see that there isn't any dangerous wiring, won't they?"

"Unless there is."

She felt the heat of anger in her cheeks. "There isn't."

"No? What if this was planned from before your arrest? What if your electrician was paid off? What if Andy did it when he went back?"

"I can't believe that!"

She heard his sharply exhaled breath. "You don't have to believe it, Arianna. Oslund doesn't have to believe it, either. He just has to believe it's possible. He has to believe a jury would consider this crime and come to the conclusion it could have been committed by somebody else."

She didn't face him, but she fought for control, conscious of his scrutiny. "That's not going to be easy, is it?"

"That depends."

"Andy thought I might be guilty." She swallowed the lump that rose with that last word. It wasn't anything she hadn't considered already. Why should it hurt to say it out loud? But it did. "He didn't go to that job to prove there was nothing wrong. He went there because he thought there might be. And he thought he might find it."

"Maybe you could give him the same courtesy, don't you think?" There was heavy irony in Cord's tone, and bitterness, but she heard what was beneath it as well. The frustration. The anger.

Beneath her crossed arms, Ari pressed her palms against her rib cage, feeling her own measure of anger, fighting it. "After my father went to prison," she said, her voice tight, "I was furious about the way my world was disrupted. I took it out on my mother, because she was there, I guess. Because she was so loyal to my father, because she never got angry herself. She just went on with her life, keeping it together, facing down all the strangers . . . and all the friends . . . who avoided her on the street, who didn't call. She said times like that were to remind you of the value of real friends. She didn't complain, and she expected the same thing of me." Ari shook her head. "I was a teenager. I thought I was the center of the universe. Once during an argument I shouted at her that maybe my father was guilty. Maybe he had stolen all that money. I was angry, and I wanted to make her angry too. She just shook her head and folded her hands together in front of her chest, in that way she had, and she said, 'Well, you're not the only one to think so. The whole jury thought so, too, and everyone else in the world, for all I know.'"

Her throat closed. Emotion filled her chest,

pressing against her control. "I never told her how sorry I was for that."

Behind her, she heard Cord cross the room to her. She could feel his closeness in the way the room seemed to still, her feelings held in thrall, suspended, waiting for him to touch her. There was pressure behind her eyes, painful emotions, human need, but she held it back, as if time had stopped for her to pass through this moment.

When she felt his hand on her shoulder, she let out her breath. Behind her closed eyelids, the tears she hadn't cried yet gathered and seeped onto her cheeks.

He let her cry. He turned her around, held her in his arms, rocked her gently back and forth, and let her cry.

It didn't last long. A burst of tears, a spate of hiccuping sobs, then she drew in a few ragged breaths and dragged her sleeve across her eyes like a young boy. She stayed wrapped in his arms, though, leaning against his chest, taking in his comfort like a balm for hurt that nothing else could soothe.

His fingers brushed the back of her neck, the side of her jaw, and he lowered his face toward hers. Without thought she raised her mouth to his and let him kiss her.

It was something other than physical touch. It was a communication of a truth she knew Cord would never let himself acknowledge in words.

"It's all right," she whispered. The words

made no sense. He was the one offering comfort. She was the one taking it. But sense didn't matter. Not to her. Not to this moment of what they shared. "It will be all right, Cord."

He held her by the shoulders, exerting enough pressure to lift her to her toes and fit his mouth across hers, the kiss suddenly hard, demanding, all-encompassing. The sounds of the city street below them, muted by the window, faded entirely as heat flared between them, fed by anger at the events they couldn't control, frustration at their suppressed need. She slid her hands down the front of his jacket and inside the lapels, circling his waist, her palms pressed against the warm, smooth cotton of his shirt.

He urged her closer, pulling her with him as he took a step back and leaned against the window casing. She felt the prodding demand of his tongue and opened her mouth for him, taking him in, welcoming the intimacy as if it were something they had shared countless times, countless ways.

Any sense of comfort given or taken vanished from between them, discarded like a pathway whose only importance was that it had brought them to this swift, deep sharing of the senses. Her tongue sought his in an impassioned dance measured by the thrumming of her heart and the shimmering, exotic pulses of need that rippled through her.

The pool game, the encounter with Oslund, their argument in the car, paled to transparency until they didn't matter. She was aware only of his warm, wet tongue, the pressure of his mouth, his hands drawing widening circles on her back, then sliding down to grasp her blouse and tug it out of her jeans.

His hands on her bare skin were strong as he circled her rib cage and his thumbs traced the lower edge of her bra. He said something against her mouth, something she couldn't understand, but the erotic vibration of his lips against hers sent her spinning even deeper into the sensuality that was filling her, melting through her. She could feel it in Cord, too, in the quicker pace of his breathing, the murmured words that came from his throat, the trembling of his hands as he unbuttoned her blouse.

His thumbs contoured the swell of her breasts, then touched her just above the front clasp of her bra. It came open in his deft hands, and his knuckles brushed her skin.

He broke off the kiss and jerked his head to one side, his breathing strident, a warm rush of air against her cheek.

A moan of response caught in her throat when he filled his hands with the weight of her breasts, his fingers caressing the outer curves, his palms warm and hard against the gathered crests, drawing a sigh of pleasure from her.

The muscles under his shirt were hard, honed, as tough and uncompromising as his presence in a courtroom, yet beneath her hands his chest rose and fell in a rapid cadence that bespoke his near loss of control.

"Arianna Rossini." His voice was a low murmur that stirred nerve endings all along her body. "You make me want things I couldn't imagine wanting before I met you." He outlined her breasts with his thumbs. "When I touch you, I don't want to stop."

She covered his hands with her own, pressing him to her, shifting her body to abrade her breasts against the rough warmth of his hands.

"Don't stop, then," she whispered.

But as if their words had switched on a light that starkly illuminated some shadowed, private, fragile being of the night, he did stop. His hands stilled, and his gaze met hers, his gray eyes vivid against the harsh, suddenly pained lines of his expression.

"Dammit, Ari," he said. "Don't you know how badly you can get hurt?"

She barely managed to whisper his name before he was gone from her, pulling away as if touch would burn them, shoving his hands into his pockets and turning his back on her.

Ari clutched at the window casing, staring blindly out through the translucent drapes at the city street, reaching for the edges of her blouse to pull it closed.

The shocking realization of his rejection poured through her, hurting, leaving her vulnerable and shaken and shamed.

Self-protective anger welled up in her and turned her toward him, a sharp, angry comment on her lips. One glance at him stopped the words. He was shaking. His back was rigid, his shoulders stiff, but no tautening of his muscles could stop the trembling.

Not looking at her, he uttered a single, gruff command: "Go, Ari."

She pulled her jacket tight around her, turned toward the door, and let herself out.

Don't you know how badly you can get hurt?

He hadn't let her answer the question. It didn't matter. It wasn't the right question anyway.

The question that mattered didn't have to do with consequences or anticipation or caution. It had to do with trust. It had to do with something that went beyond the dictates of the law, the ethics of a profession. It went beyond reasonable doubt. It went all the way to the truth of her innocence.

And Cord had never asked that question.

EIGHT

Hurt, humiliated, rejected, Ari got through the following days without him.

Andy didn't come to work. When he called, she didn't ask him why, beyond a cursory inquiry about whether he was all right. He told her yes.

One of her clients abruptly canceled a job, offering no excuse. She didn't ask him why, either.

Victor worked overtime to finish the project Andy would have done, and made no comment about the lost job that was to have provided part of their future income. Ari let all of it go too. Dealing with the present was all she could do right now. The future was an unknown being that lurked in wait around the next crisis.

It came soon enough. Pulling into her driveway two days after she'd last seen Cord, Ari parked beside a car she didn't recognize. Carefully avoiding speculation, not wanting to acknowledge the fears she'd been fighting, she walked into the house.

The silence alerted her—an odd gathering of the air that crumbled her protective numbness like the blow of a hammer.

On the hall chair was a leather briefcase, black, the corners tipped with brass, not new but of a quality that didn't show wear. The clasp had a lock on it. The case was long enough for legal briefs.

In the living room, her father was sitting in his favorite easy chair, his back straight, his hands gripping the armrests as if they were weapons. Charlie Kent was standing beside the fireplace with his hands in the pockets of his pressed tweed trousers, his jacket open and his tie loose, disheveled and suave as always. On his face, though, was an expression of frowning worry, as if he didn't know what to make of Pop and couldn't fathom how to begin. He turned toward her with an air of relief, as if she could solve this problem, straighten everything out.

She let her purse slide off her shoulder onto the oak table just inside the room.

"Arianna," he said, when she didn't greet him.

She nodded. "Charlie."

He didn't step toward her, and he kept his hands in his pockets. He looked like he could have used something to hold, to cover the awkwardness of not offering to shake hands. She could smell coffee in the kitchen, but Pop, it seemed, hadn't offered Charlie a cup. It occurred to her that Pop hadn't invited him to sit down, either.

Charlie's mouth twitched in a slight, ironic grin that could have been a comment on her thoughts. "You've done a lot with the house, you and your father," he said, glancing around the room, trying to bridge the tension with conversation. "A lot has changed since I was here last."

"Yes. It's been quite a few years." Since before Pop got out of prison, she thought, when Charlie Kent had come to see how they were getting along. Her mother had told him, pridefully, standing in this room, that they were fine.

"You know," Charlie continued, "I pass on your name whenever I have the chance to recommend a carpenter. I know the quality of your work. I always have."

"Thank you," she said. "Some of this is Pop's work. We did it together."

"Yes. Well." Charlie looked around again, nodding.

Pop still said nothing. His face was set and stony, his eyes level but unreadable when they met hers. Charlie had never visited after Pop came home. She wasn't sure why. It was one of the things connected to that time in his life he wouldn't talk about.

"I know your father is retired," Charlie said, looking back at her. "But it's nice that you have this chance to work here—when you can work together."

"Yes."

He pulled one hand out of his pocket and rested his arm on the mantel, his forearm dangling loose, consciously casual. "You're partners in working on the house. That's good sometimes, to have a partner. That way, if one of you makes a mistake, the other one can cover for you. It's what partners are for."

"My daughter doesn't make mistakes in her work!" Pop's voice was irritable.

"No," Charlie agreed. "I can see that. Not in her carpentry."

Pop tightened his grip on the arms of the chair until his knuckles turned white. Ari took a step toward him, one hand outspread to calm him.

"Why don't you just come out and say what you mean to say?" She turned toward Charlie, squaring her shoulders, feeling a rising anger that matched the animosity already in the room. "If you're here to talk about your partner, just say what you came for."

"Yeah, I guess I should." He gave her a worldly, friendly shrug. "I'm here to offer my services, Arianna, if you decide you want another lawyer."

"She has a lawyer," Pop said. "Why would she want another one?"

Charlie sighed, fiddling with the button of his suit jacket. "Maybe you didn't hear that my partner socked the D.A. in the jaw the other day."

Her father shot Ari a glance. "Maybe he deserved it," Pop said.

"Nevertheless, it wasn't a good move."

Ari felt incredulity, outrage, and sheer distaste forming like a tangled ball of wire in her chest. Cord had said Charlie was *family*. A friend. "Why aren't you telling this to your partner," she snapped, her voice taut, "instead of to me?"

"Because I don't want to see you pay for it." Charlie shook his head, his mouth curved in a rueful smile that set Ari's teeth on edge. "He's too close to this, Arianna," he said quietly. "He's letting it get personal."

"What's personal?" Pop challenged, pushing himself up from the chair. "He's on my daughter's side. That's what he thinks. This is too personal for you?"

"Pop—"

"The point is," Charlie went on, standing his ground, "that personal involvement is not good tactics."

"Not good tactics! Not good tactics? Whose side should he be on, then? The judge's? The jury's?"

"That's not what I said, Tomas."

No, Ari thought. And not what he meant, either. He meant Cord should be on no one's side but his own. The way Charlie was.

"What I'm trying to say," Charlie went on, "is that my services are available to your daughter if she wants them. I just wanted you to be informed of your options."

Just wanted you to be informed. Without thought to who it might hurt, or what loyalties it might betray. Charlie Kent didn't think in those terms. A picture of him she hadn't seen before took form in her mind. Her hand rose unconsciously to the cameo she wore around her throat. "You're the one who called Pop, aren't you?" she said slowly. "When I was arrested. No one in my crew would have done that. It was you."

"Yes," Charlie said. "I thought he should know."

"No matter how much it worried him? Did you give a thought to that? Or was that too *personal* to consider?"

Charlie pushed his hands into his pockets again, sighed, and gave her his faint, charming, ironic grin. "It's a serious mistake to get too personal, Arianna. You know, I played soccer with your father. He could tell you—when you start worrying about your teammates' feelings, whether they'll be hurt if you don't pass to them, whether your girlfriend has a thing for the halfback—you lose sight of the goal. And then you lose the game. You don't want to lose this game."

She said nothing, her jaw clenched. Finally he turned, walked through their living room, and let himself out.

Ari sank down onto the chair in front of her,

propped her elbows on her knees and covered her face with her hands.

"So what is he going to do?" Pop asked. "This lawyer of yours. He has a plan?"

She shook her head. "I don't know."

"You don't know? What? What?" Pop demanded.

"I don't know!"

"All right, all right," Pop muttered. "That's up to the lawyer, huh? Not to the likes of me."

She lowered her hands to look at him.

"Did he do that—hit the D.A. in the jaw?"

"Yes."

Pop nodded. "Over you? Over whether you were guilty?"

"Over something to do with the case."

"What?"

"Nothing, Pop. It doesn't matter."

"What was it, that doesn't matter?"

"Nothing."

Pop tipped his head back, peering at her, his eyes blazing. "He thinks you did this, or not?"

Her throat tight, Ari shook her head. "We haven't talked about it."

Pop slashed the air with one hand, twisting it at the wrist in a disgusted gesture. "What have you talked about, then? You don't talk about the truth. You don't know what the lawyer is going to do for you. Maybe you don't want to think about it. Is that it?"

"Maybe it is, Pop."

"Yes. And maybe you don't want to look at it, either. Maybe it's what he said." Instead of saying Charlie's name, he gestured toward the door where Charlie had disappeared. "You're running real fast in the wrong direction. Maybe you should listen to him, then, if you don't want to listen to me."

"Pop—"

"What?" Demanding. Belligerent. Stubborn.

And unanswerable. Like all the other threatening, weighted, and unanswered questions in her life.

Ari stood up abruptly. "I'm going out."

The clipped statement, like something from a rebellious teenager, silenced Pop. She let it stand. It was what she felt like—rebellious, confused, faced with demands she should be able to answer when she had no answers to give him. "I won't be here for dinner."

"Ahh." Pop waved a disgusted hand at her as she turned and walked to the hall. "I won't make dinner," he called as she pulled open the front door.

She closed it behind her, went down the stairs, and got into her truck. She started the engine, then stopped for a moment, her head down on the steering wheel, protest and pain welling up in her chest.

Old pain, but as sharp and piercing and bright as when she'd been fifteen and full of anguish, wanting to hurt someone as she was hurting herself.

This time she'd thought she had it figured out, how to protect the people she loved. How to cheat the injustice and the anger. She was wrong. Other forces were pushing at her, defiant, brazen, careless of who would be hurt. Pop . . . Andy . . . Victor . . . and Cord, blindsided by a partner he'd thought of as family.

She squeezed her eyes shut, locking her jaw against the acknowledgment. She hadn't wanted anybody to be accused in her place. Cord's stark, factual structuring of reasonable doubt out of the lives of people she loved and trusted had left her chilled to the bone, cold and sickened.

Maybe the only answer was the truth. The facts. Finding out who was guilty. Maybe it was time she needed to know that.

Fifteen minutes later she pulled up in front of Cord's office. Her truck parked at the curb, she sat with her hands draped over the top of the steering wheel, staring at the darkened and quiet building.

It was after hours. And this one night, anyway, Cord wasn't there.

Her throat got tight again, then the building blurred. Without the conscious permission of her will, she was crying, her cheeks wet, her hands clenched into fists on the dashboard.

She wasn't sure how long she sat there, or what made her wipe her eyes and look around, but

the sense of *something wrong*, something out of
sync, straightened her back and made her peer
again at the wooden Victorian structure and its
twin across the parking lot—the building she'd
been renovating.

There was no movement, no light behind the
tall windows, nothing out of place on the wide
porch. But under the eaves, fine gray wisps of
smoke were escaping into the clear, still evening.
Smoke.

Clutching the dashboard, sitting up straighter,
she imagined she could smell it. That wooden
building—the "faulty wiring" that Oslund had
claimed was there—the sickening, obvious conclusion about smoke under the eaves.

Galvanized into action, Ari reached for her car
phone and pressed the emergency number, then
muttered, "Come on!" at the short delay before it
was answered. When she heard the voice, she
snapped into the receiver, "A fire. 75 Chestnut
Street. Yellow Victorian. Unoccupied. Hurry!"

She slammed the phone down, threw her
weight against the door of the truck, and was running toward the building before she'd had time to
analyze her actions. Just inside the front door was
a fire extinguisher, as clearly placed in her mind as
the workings of her own house. It was a builder's
instinct that drove her, even more than the practi-
cal knowledge that any fire caused by wiring
would be slow to start and easily stopped, and that
any evidence of arson would be shown only if it

was stopped. This was her renovation that was threatened—her plans, her craftsmanship, her artisan's work—and the idea that someone would burn it down sparked a blaze of pure, hot anger.

She ripped aside the police barrier and yanked at the front door. It was locked. With strength borne of determination, she tore a three-foot scaffolding board from its tacks on the porch railing and smashed the glass in the front door, then reached through and turned the knob.

Most of the smoke was in the back room, but enough of it drifted lazily toward the front hall, swirling in eddies from the air current of the open door. It should have set off the smoke alarm. She couldn't understand why it hadn't.

Ari grabbed the extinguisher, peering into the back room toward the electrical box where all the wires came together, where an electrical fire would logically start, where the smoke was gathered.

The explosion slammed her back against the front door, the extinguisher crashing against the glass. A flash of dull red light, then a wave of heat hit her like a fist, and pain shot through her wrist where her hand had smashed into the door.

Gasping, she stumbled out onto the porch and down the stairs onto the lawn, then turned her shocked gaze back to the house.

Flames were glowing behind the windows, red, eerie, alive.

A siren screamed in the distance, summoned

by the flames. As it grew louder and the fire truck slowed at the curb, Ari turned her head and stared at the flashing lights—two sets of red, then one set of blue. She was still standing on the lawn when the firemen rushed past her and the policeman took her arm.

Cord found her amidst the smoke and the confusion, the shouts of the workmen, the blast of static from the police loudspeakers. She was sitting in her truck, her head tipped back against the seat rest, her eyes closed.

Relieved, angry, his nerves taut with worry, he yanked open the door with enough violence to make her jump. "Dammit, Ari. They said there was an explosion. Someone told me you were in the building when it happened."

She blinked at him. The skin was drawn tight over her cheekbones, bleached of color except for the pulsing blue light of the police car. Her dark eyes looked enormous in her white face.

Guilt shot through him. He let out a breath and tipped his head down to the roof of the truck, his shoulders sagging, his arms draped between the door and the frame. "Are you all right?"

She nodded.

"What the hell were you doing there?" he asked.

"I saw the smoke. I thought it must be what Oslund said—some wires set up to cause a fire.

There's nothing there to really burn so fast. I thought I could put it out."

He swore again, the words graphic and uncensored, fear and frustration obvious in the tone.

When he looked at her, her mouth was curved in a faint, wry grin, willful, brave, defiant. "For a lawyer, you know a lot of gutter language," she said.

"Yes, I do. And since I met you, I've been inspired."

She gave a small, almost soundless humph. "Have you? You talk a good line, but you don't ever seem to do much of anything about it."

His ironic smile solidified into something that wasn't quite a smile, as if it would break the clenched muscles of his face. He had a sudden urge to reach inside the truck and pull her up against him, to drive his tongue into her mouth and his hands into her shirt and demonstrate just how "much of anything" he was capable of doing that would make his gutter language sound like schoolyard prattle.

She was watching him now, intently. Two delicate pink-tinted streaks had appeared in her cheeks, contrasting with the fair skin and gold hair.

He'd replayed that scene in his office fifty times in the past two days, all the time cursing himself for the distraction he couldn't afford while he was pouring over records in the courthouse, interviewing a recalcitrant and surly apprentice carpenter, or pumping three cops from Garza's department for useful information.

None of it had dimmed the intensity of his obsession with Ari. None of it had touched him a tenth as deeply as the pure, raw panic he'd felt when he'd stared at the burning building and someone beside him had asked about the woman who'd been inside.

"You haven't told me what you were doing here," he said.

She looked down for just a second. "I was watching your office." She raised her hand to brush an errant curl of hair away from her forehead, and he felt another shock of reaction, uncontrolled, out of reality. There was a jagged gash of torn flesh across the back of her arm.

"What the hell happened to you?" he said harshly.

She glanced at the wound. "It's not serious. My arm hit the glass."

My arm hit the glass. Casual. Unimportant.

The thought of her hurt, in danger, tore through him like the devouring flames he'd seen minutes earlier in the burning building. He'd made up his mind how he would treat her, the distance he had to keep. But he hadn't counted on her being in danger, hurt, threatened by something that had taken on the sinister color of malice.

He pulled the door wider. "Come on. I'll take you to have it looked at."

She shook her head, not moving to accommodate him on the seat. "The police asked me to wait. They want to question me."

He shut his eyes for a moment, gritting his teeth, wrapped in an anger too profound to analyze. "They can wait."

Her face was a study in unguarded innocence, clear reality, simple truth. "For what?" she said softly.

Cord swore again, silently, the curse aimed at himself, at his own savage urge to take the innocence that she offered, as if there were no consequences to that offer.

She had no sense of self-protection, no instinct for self-interest. *I can handle the truth*, she'd told him. As if it couldn't hurt her.

"I've had you in my mind for days, Ari, wondering where you were. What you were doing. Whether you were okay. I didn't call you because I told myself you were okay. I never once thought you'd be here, in that damned building, when it was about to blow."

She smiled again, so slightly. "You told me to leave," she said. "You didn't tell me where I should go."

His gaze met hers, and the jolt he felt jarred him to the bones. "What happened," he asked, "that you needed to talk to me?"

"Charlie came to see us."

"My partner?"

She nodded. "He told me you couldn't handle

my case. You were too involved. You couldn't be objective. He offered to take over."

Cord straightened slowly, resting his clenched fist on the top of the door, his mind calling up an image of Charlie in his office that morning.

You want some help on this thing, Cord?

No, he'd said. *I can handle it.*

"What'd you tell him?" he asked Ari.

She didn't need to answer. The startled puzzlement that crossed her face was enough.

"Why not?" he asked, compelled to push it. "Charlie's a good lawyer. Maybe that would be the smartest thing you could do."

Her eyes met his with a directness that went straight to the bone. "Because I didn't like what he was doing behind your back."

Cord's fist clenched a little tighter.

"And because he thinks I'm guilty."

He didn't bother to say it didn't matter, that none of it mattered, that no lawyer's job required that he have absolute loyalty to his law partner or that he believe in innocence. Cord had gone beyond the logic, the reasoning. He'd gone beyond understanding his own motives with Ari. Maybe beyond control of them.

"I drove here . . . to see you . . ."

She stopped and took a breath. This was hard for her, he realized, and the thought brought another reaction burning through him—the impulse to protect her, to gather her against him and block out whatever threatened her.

"Ari—"

She raised her chin. "Because I needed to know what happened. I thought I could keep myself out of it. I thought I didn't have to know what really happened. That it was just me who was involved. But I realized tonight it wasn't just me. It's Pop and Andy . . . and you."

The strange and unfamiliar emotion that went through him felt like an electric current wired to his heart.

She glanced down. "And I thought . . . what I'm doing to you . . . maybe it's too much to ask."

The words were barely a whisper. She held herself still, the way she had the first time he'd seen her in the superior court holding cell. The pulsing blue light flickered over her face, washing the color from her hair. Caught in the surreal light, she looked ethereal, insubstantial as light and shadow, the real flesh-and-blood woman lost in the nightmare where she'd found herself.

Slowly and deliberately, Cord let go of the door and reached out to touch her. She looked up, startled, when his fingers brushed back a lock of her hair. She caught her bottom lip in her teeth, but when he laid his palm against her jaw, his fingers twining into her hair, her mouth softened into the unconscious shape of a question.

In answer, he cupped the other side of her jaw, framing her face with his hands, and leaned into the truck, tipping her face up.

Her lips were warm, damp, soft, tasting faintly of smoke and salt. She'd been crying.

Driven by an urge he couldn't name, he twisted his head to take her mouth in a kiss that parted her lips and laid claim to the secret inner surfaces and erased the taste of smoke and tears.

When he lifted his head, her lips were pink and glistening, and there were two bright streaks across her pale cheeks, defying the garish blue light. His heart was beating like a trip-hammer.

"Don't go anywhere," he said, his voice a hoarse rasp of command. "I have to talk to the police. And then I'm taking you home."

NINE

Caught in a swirl of emotion she had no time to process, Ari watched Cord walk across the lawn toward a policeman standing beside the driver of one of the fire trucks. Firemen were restacking hose, moving more slowly now that the fire was controlled and the crisis was over. The policeman greeted Cord as he approached, then smiled at something he said. Ari thought she recognized him as the man who had guarded her cell. She couldn't remember his name.

Cord said something that made both men glance toward her truck, then he lifted his hand, touching his forearm. He was obviously explaining about her injury. He turned in a moment and walked back toward her.

The little jump in her heart made no sense. There was no logic in it, just feeling—humming, expectant, half alarmed.

He reached the open door of her truck. "I told the police your arm needs to be attended to," he said. "They can talk to you in the morning."

She nodded, but didn't move. She was aware that he wanted something more of her, but her thoughts were scattered, and she couldn't seem to pull them together.

He said gently, "I'll drive, Ari."

"Oh. Yes." She slid over on the seat to let him get in beside her.

Awkwardly, a little inept at maneuvering her truck, he backed up to the police car behind them and pulled out into the street. They didn't speak until he'd driven around the fire trucks and pulled away from the scene. A policeman gazed after them. Ari looked away, wondering what the officer thought of her leaving with Cord driving her truck, his tie loose and his suit jacket off.

She had no idea what the man would think. She had no idea what she thought herself. She didn't seem to be thinking much—only noticing. The way his hair fanned over his collar, disheveled and thick and soft. The set of his jaw, clamped tight with determination and concern. The strength of his wrist where it rested on the bottom of the steering wheel.

"Where are we going?" she asked him.

He glanced at her. "Your call, Ari. If you want to go to the emergency room or your own doctor, that's fine. But my upstairs neighbor is a paramedic, and I know she's home. She'd bandage your arm if you wanted her to."

She watched him adjust the mirror, then glance down at the gearshift to slow for a light. "Where do you live?" she asked.

He glanced at her again, clearly surprised. "Off Salisbury. I have an apartment in one of the old town houses. I thought you knew."

"How would I?"

"I don't know." He smiled, a funny quirk of his lips, a little lopsided. "Look it up in the court records, I suppose."

She felt herself smile in return, in spite of the nervous, jumpy tangle of reactions inside her. "The lawyer's way," she said. "It seems like a lot of trouble when you could just ask."

He didn't respond. He would have told her he couldn't trust the answers, she thought. He was a lawyer. He had to have proof.

Maybe she did too. Maybe she'd wanted him to kiss her. Maybe that was what she'd been asking for, trying to tell him.

The tangled emotions expanded, pressed at her from the inside, tripping her heart into higher rhythm.

She was used to knowing what she wanted, knowing her future. But her future wasn't clear or solid anymore. It was just broken boards and splintered wood and this unsettled, urgent need inside her.

"Are you all right?" he asked her. "Is your arm

all right?" The question was sharp. She must have looked distraught.

"Yes. Fine." To her surprise, her voice sounded normal. Almost normal, anyway. "My arm is fine. It's just an arm."

He looked at her again, askance.

"Not a hand," she explained. "When you work with your hands, that's the part of yourself you're careful of."

He stared at her a moment, then smiled again. This time the expression was wry. "I guess when you're a lawyer, you tend to think you should be careful of all parts."

All parts. Hands. Hearts. Illusions. She didn't think so. She didn't think they were going to be careful. She didn't want to be. And maybe he'd gone past wanting to be too. Maybe for him it was this same demanding, clamoring need that wouldn't listen to the idea of being careful.

He made a turn onto a residential street. This was the old, well-heeled part of the city, the streets tree lined and set with old Victorians like a gathering of large and graceful matrons bejeweled with lights just coming on in the windows. The glimpses of interiors, warm with wood and lamplight, made the street feel familiar to her, like her own.

Cord's building was rambling, turreted, and shingled, the recently landscaped grounds planted with young trees that looked naked and vulnerable against the fading pearl of the sky. The new green of their budding branches was invisible in the dusk, but along the walkway forsythia bushes had started to bloom, their yellow blossoms paled to almost white in the fading light.

She hadn't thought about him apart from his office, she realized. She hadn't put him in any setting besides the ones she'd seen, places different from her own world because they were so imbued with his profession.

Maybe they weren't so different, she thought, she and Cord.

She had an unsettling sense of a shifting point of view, like looking at an optical illusion print. If she blinked, she might see it differently, be unable to go back to seeing it the first way.

He pulled the truck into a numbered parking space behind the house, and glanced toward it. "My neighbor's light is on," he said. "So she's home." He got out of the truck, putting her keys in his pocket, and came around to open her door before she'd pulled up the handle.

He touched the small of her back, guiding her along the forsythia-lined walkway to the deep porch, making the simple act of walking into the building intimate. Secret, shivery sensations flickered along her spine.

Nita Hagstrom's apartment was on the second floor, off a paneled landing at the top of wide stairs. A tall, gray-haired woman in jeans and a pink sweatshirt answered the door and greeted

Cord with pleased surprise, then ushered them into her apartment.

She brushed off Cord's appreciation for her services and clucked over Ari's arm, dabbing at the wound with antiseptic and sterile compress.

"How'd you do this, honey?" she asked, sympathetic and humorous. "You trip over some of Cord's law books downstairs?"

"No." Ari hesitated, then said, "I was in a building where there was an explosion. My arm went through the glass of the door."

Nita Hagstrom stopped swabbing for a moment, eyebrows raised. "Downtown?" she asked. "The office building, this evening?"

Cord made a sound in the back of his throat, glancing at her, shifting his weight and pushing his hands into his pockets. His lawyer's instinct wasn't comfortable with her saying it right out, she thought. She had an absurd image of them all in a bad gangster movie, where she'd be stitched up on the kitchen table, no doctor, don't-tell-the-police.

She looked at him, amused at her own whimsy, and it occurred to her that the emotion was real: The sense of danger, the uncertainty about what would happen next. She was with Cord Prescott, in the place where he lived, because he'd released her from her commitment elsewhere until morning.

"There you go, honey," Nita Hagstrom said,

taping the bandage in place. "Should be okay.
Keep your arm out of glass doors, all right?"

"Yes. Thank you."

The woman ushered them out into the hallway, smiled good night, and shut the door, leaving
them alone. Against the bare wooden floor and
the white painted walls, Cord's dark-suited presence seemed overwhelmingly real to her, substantive, every detail imprinted on her senses—the
scent of expensive wool and the brush of his hands
in his pockets; the intense gray gaze, serious,
searching, sharing, she thought, that sense of danger and need she'd felt in Nita's apartment.

"You look like you could use a drink," he said
finally. "Come downstairs and I'll give you one."

It was a simple enough offer, a way to avoid
making a decision, she thought, between going
home and staying there. The odd sense of inevita-
bility crept into her reactions again. Like a doorway, she thought. If she walked through it, she
wouldn't be able to go back.

She followed him down the stairs. He unlocked his door and led her into a spacious,
sparsely furnished room, bare of all but the most
essential furniture: A sofa, two chairs, an end table, and, as Nita Hagstrom had suggested, piles of
books overspilling the single low bookcase along
one wall, stacked on top of the bookcase, the
floor, the end table. But the room was immacu-
late, the ornate woodwork gleaming with polish,
the floor freshly waxed. She wandered across the

room to the window and ran her fingers along the elaborately carved casing, the custom-fitted wooden blinds.

"Is it up to your standards, Arianna Rossini?"

She nodded. That sense of taking a potential, inevitable step washed over her once more. "I don't know," she said.

Frowning, he stared at the window casing.

She let out a huff of uncertain laughter. "No, I didn't mean that. I meant . . ." She trailed off, the words fading into silence, replaced by a consciousness of him that idle conversation couldn't dissipate. He was looking at her in that way that was so compelling—the way that had become familiar to her, as if he would consider her for as long as it took until he could see through to the truth.

What he would do with that truth she didn't know.

His voice, a little hoarse, broke the silence. "I'll get you that drink. What would you like?"

She shrugged. "Wine. Beer. Whatever."

"I have some wine in the kitchen. Would you like that?"

She nodded, then watched him disappear into an adjacent room where he switched on a light. The yellow rectangle spilled into the living room, sharply defined against the wooden floor, making her aware of the shadows in the rest of the room.

Cord came back with a stemmed glass, handed it to her, then stood watching her while she sipped it. She felt warmth creep into her cheeks as she wondered how she looked to him, in her jeans and a chamois shirt, her face free of makeup. The thought that he'd kissed her flicked across her mind, bringing its own wash of heat, its own nervous quiver of uncertainty.

"Will you have trouble over this?" she asked him. "With Charlie?"

He let out a breath. "Yes. It won't be new. He told me this morning he didn't think I should be handling your case."

". . . Oh."

"I told him it wasn't his call. He must have decided it was yours."

"I wouldn't have thought he had any right to make that kind of decision."

Cord's expression hardened. "I don't know what he figured it was. A gratuitous offer to one of my clients isn't his usual style."

"Because it's disloyal?" There was a note of accusation in her words.

She thought he wasn't going to answer. When he spoke, his voice was hard. "I don't know. I guess I'm not sure where Charlie's loyalties lie. Maybe I never was."

"He's your partner."

He raked his fingers through his hair, his jaw clenched, then met her gaze again. "Nothing about this makes sense, Arianna. Not the case, not my partner, not you and me."

No, it didn't, she thought. Least of all Cord

and her. "That's why I'm here, then?" she said. "To make sense of it?"

He didn't answer her. There was no answer. No answer that made sense. Not in words, anyway.

"I told myself I wouldn't let this happen again," he said.

"I know."

Silence filtered in after her words. Ari glanced down at her glass to avoid his eyes.

The wine was dry, tart. Probably expensive, but not to her liking. She set the glass on the windowsill and shifted her gaze to the window, where tall, arching forsythia branches filtered the fading light into lacy patterns against the glass.

She heard him take a step closer to her, standing behind her, making her heart quicken in her tight chest, but she didn't turn around.

"Do you want me to take you home, Arianna?"

She was silent for a moment, gathering herself. "I don't know," she said finally, facing him. She crossed her arms in front of her and looked up at him. "How far are you going to let things go before you send me home anyway?"

He pushed his hands into his pockets, as if to stop himself from touching her, but his dark gaze flicked over her face, her lips, her throat, as if the touch had already been made. "If you intend to go home, Ari," he said, "you'd better do it now."

A tiny, bright thread of panic shot through

her, her chest, her throat, her heart, singing in her blood like something outside her, some wind rushing past her ears. What she felt for him, she thought with sudden, meticulous focus, was the kind of emotion that could splinter the framework of her life.

He pulled a hand out of his pocket and reached up to touch her throat. His index finger traced the inside of her collar, cool, smooth, until he touched the gold chain she wore around her neck. His fingers followed it to the cameo hanging just inside the second button of her shirt, just above her breasts.

She drew in a quick breath and held it, transfixed by his touch.

"Was this your mother's?" he asked.

"Yes." She covered his hand with her own, holding him there, keeping him from moving again.

His gaze flicked up from her throat to her eyes, penetrating any defenses she might have. "Will you stay?" he asked.

She couldn't move for a moment, then the word formed in her mind, in her throat, on her lips. "Yes."

She felt him absorb the word as if he were watching the disintegration of some wall that had been between them. Like the finest glass, it shattered into countless pieces, dissipated like the resistance in an electric field when the opposite poles had been shut off.

His hand moved again, tracing the outline of the cameo, touching her through the warm, carved stone.

"Do you look like her?" he asked. "Your mother? Did she have reddish-blond hair and brown eyes?" His fingers left the necklace and touched her eyebrow, tracing the curve of it with his fingertip. "And blond eyebrows?"

She shook her head. "She was fair, but I don't look like her. We're alike in other ways."

He took her hand and brought it to his mouth. He didn't kiss it, but he touched it, just barely, to his lips. His breath was a warm, moist drift against her knuckles, then he turned her hand over. His tongue flicked in the hollow of her thumb, then along the heel of her hand, then in the center of her palm.

Her breath caught, ragged, releasing her heart to beat faster, tripping over itself.

"I was in my office tonight," he murmured, his eyes meeting hers over the tips of her fingers, his lips making patterns in her palm. "I was in the computer room. And I was thinking of you. Why didn't you come up?"

"I was afraid to," she said. "I had to figure out first what I'd say."

"Afraid of what happened the last time?" He brought their clasped hands back to her throat and traced with his knuckle a line that loosened the next button of her shirt.

When he'd touched her before, it had been a

swift capitulation to an impulse that carried them both past thought. This was different. She could feel the tension in his hand, his body, the exquisitely agonizing discipline of making this act mindful and deliberate.

"The first time I saw you, Ari, in jail . . . I wanted to do this. I knew it was impossible, but I couldn't believe in the impossibility. Do you know what that's like?"

She knew what it was like for him. She'd felt it. She could feel it now. "Like being at war with yourself. Two sides, fighting."

His hand dipped lower, and his gaze followed it. He released her hand and unfastened the next button of her shirt, just over the center clasp of her bra. "Both sides wanted you," he said.

He brought his lips down to brush her mouth, just touching it, drawing back even while she would have pressed closer to him. He bent his head to her neck, the pulse at the juncture of her collarbone, then lower, to the cleft between her breasts.

Her eyes slid shut. Rivulets of sensation washed out from the center of her chest where his mouth touched her, to the peaks of her breasts and the hollow of her stomach.

He took her hands from where she'd clasped his waist and brought them up between them, to the open collar of her shirt.

She expected him to unbutton her shirt, but instead he let go of her hands and shrugged off his jacket. He dropped it on the windowsill, then, still with his eyes on her, fumbled for the cord of the blinds and pulled the slats shut, closing out the last of the fading light, closing them into dim, shadowed privacy.

He cupped the side of her neck and hooked his thumb into the gold chain.

Her hands were still raised between them, her fingers brushing the placket of his shirt. She could unbutton it. The image of undressing him, seeing him naked, drew her, tugging at her senses.

Her hands were shaking too badly to do it. She flattened her palms on his chest, then slid her hands down the front of his shirt to his waist, grasped his shirt, and pulled it out of his pants.

He went still, waiting, but sucked in his breath when she slipped her shaking finger inside his belt and fumbled at the catch.

She couldn't unfasten it. The hands that could shape wood as if it were alive, coax intricate magic from tool and material, couldn't loosen the brass buckle on a leather belt.

Her throat closed around a small sound of fierce panic and her hands fisted around the buckle.

Cord cupped the back of her head and tipped her face up, then brought his mouth down on hers, hard. With tongue and lips and hands he engaged her mouth, her emotions, her focus. When he lifted his mouth from hers, he pushed his fingers deeper into her hair, holding the back of her head with savage purpose.

"What scares you?" he asked, his voice low and rough and demanding. "Tell me. Say it."

She swallowed. "I'm afraid of . . . what's going to happen. Losing control. Not being able to get it back again. I never wanted to hurt anyone, and I'm afraid of—" She clenched her jaw, forcing back a heavy lump in her throat. "Of hurting people I care about."

"Listen to me, Arianna." He wrapped her upper arms in the strong grip of his hands, lifting her shoulders. "Nothing like that is going to happen. You're not going to jail. I won't let—"

"Don't." Her voice was sharp enough to stop him, fierce enough to carry conviction. "Don't make promises like that. You don't know if they're true."

"Ari." His hands gripped tighter. "I'll do everything I can. I'll make it come out—"

"No." This time her voice was softer, with a catch of pain in it, and she stopped him with her fingers against his lips. "No, Cord. You mustn't play with the truth. It will hurt you. You can't—" She had to stop and take a breath while he threaded his hands into her hair again, his face contorted. "You can't make it different," she got out. "You can't control it, either."

Tension hardened the muscles in his shoulders, his chest, his thighs. "What will you let me give you, then? What will you take?"

She brushed his mouth with hers, seeking, finding. "Just this," she whispered.

She felt the sharp exhalation of his breath, then his thumbs erased the wet tracks that angled down her cheeks. He pressed his mouth against her eyelids, her nose, then her lips once more. "Dear God," he said, "don't ask me to take you home."

"Don't take me home," she whispered.

"No . . ." The word was a gruff murmur against her mouth, then his tongue sought entry. The kiss was fevered, ardent, and all-consuming, heated with an arousal swift enough and deep enough to vanquish her doubts and dissipate her panic. With a half-murmured sigh she gave herself to the only truth she could hold in her mind.

His mouth moved against hers, warm and moist, soft and then hard, enticing her into exploring the pleasure, the sweet heat they made between them. Hungry for him, her body already heavy with desire too urgent to deny, she threaded her hands into his hair and gave herself to this choice, this act.

Holding her, still kissing her, he turned them as if they were locked in some slow, erotic dance and walked her back toward the sofa. The white linen was striped by pale thin bands of light from the blinds that roped over their tangled limbs as he lowered her down, half on, half off the loose cushions while he braced one knee on the floor beside her.

"Do that again, Arianna." He combed his hands through her hair. "Touch me. Touch me the way I've thought about it."

But it was Cord's hands that were magic, whispering against her skin as they unfastened her chamois shirt, then hesitating, hovering over the peach-colored lace of her bra as if in ritual, warm with promise and reverence. She waited, breathless, for him to cup her breasts, but he slipped his hands under her back, supporting her, lifting her, and touched the center of the lace with just his lips, an intimacy that made her sigh out a wordless and needful sound.

He'd seen her aroused, passionate, but not like this, unguarded, willingly responsive, utterly feminine in that response.

Pulling her under him, he unclasped the bra, his hands on her skin, his face buried in the fragrant cloud of her hair. His fingers in the hollow of her spine, he arched her body to fit with his, searching out the fullness that matched the contours of his hips, his thighs.

Hungry for the intimate contact of her skin, he unzipped her jeans and pushed them down her hips.

She answered the seeking pressure of his hand with sweet and mindless response, opening with the pulse of her need. He pressed his palm against the softness of her inner thigh, then circled her buttocks, parting her thighs to fit her against him.

She had told him, articulately, every time they

had met before this, what she wanted from him, how she would let him serve her, but now their communication was the murmur of incoherent passion, the language of hands and bodies. She pulled away his shirt, and he answered her with his own meaningless words, his own hand unsnapping and unzipping his pants.

"I've wanted you to do this, Cord," she whispered in a caught breath. "I've wanted this."

"This?" he murmured. He hooked his thumbs into the delicate lace of her panties. "You've wanted this?"

"Yes. That. Yes."

The pace of their breathing grew more urgent, demanding fulfillment that they deferred, extending the foreplay, postponing the completion of this act.

He stopped long enough to look at her, touching her with his hands as his eyes took in the slim strength of her workman's body, her fair, smooth skin, like fine damask. He kissed the small bruise on the back of her arm above the bandage, her wrist where the handcuff marks had been, the calluses on her palm, then traced with his mouth the faint marks left from her bra on the undersides of her breasts.

He'd wondered if she'd be self-conscious of the body she concealed with boyish work clothes and the conservative suit she'd worn to court, if she'd be virginal in her responses, shy, a product of her father's protectiveness. But she let him undress her, touch her, with no consciousness of herself that was separate from the two of them together. She murmured what she wanted from him and what she wanted to do in the same breath, her brown eyes catching his with shimmering desire.

"Now," she whispered. "Come inside me. I want you." Her hands circled his hips and guided him toward her, close to her, into her, until they were completed, joined together.

Cord held himself still, poised above her, hands in her hair, elbows sunk deep into the cushions beside her shoulders. Her dark gold hair haloed her face—the flush of passion across her cheekbones, the pink, passion-full mouth, the dark eyes rimmed in gold, open wide, trusting, letting him in. Her mouth curved, then formed words that he heard as if they came from somewhere inside his head.

Kiss me.

His mouth found hers in the near darkness. He started to move, then the sounds were the rhythmic brush of skin against linen, breath against breath, body to body, a growl deep in his throat that was hungry, possessive, the elemental acknowledgment and acclaim of bonding.

Her hands clutched his shoulders, his held the back of her head as he moved within her, locking their mouths in a kiss that burned with heat, with passion, with the thrusting, driving beat of their bodies matching rhythm and force, giving and taking, striving together toward that uncharted fall through the spaces of sense and mind.

Holding back, fighting for control, Cord heard her say something she couldn't have said, something that had no words, an urging to let go.

"Come with me," he countered, his voice rough, urgent.

With breathless emotion, half demand, half capitulation, she whispered, "Take me there." Then she tore her mouth away from his and he was listening to her cry of completion, pouring himself into her, losing himself in sweet, uncharted ecstasy. He'd been willing to fling his soul to the darkness, not knowing what lost place he'd be in afterward, but around their joining the darkness was lit by a burst of shining, star-sprinkled light that left no room for anything but joy.

Locked together, trembling, murmuring words whose meaning didn't matter, they drifted down together from that bright, explosive summit, mindless of the scattered couch cushions, the strewn clothes, their own shared abandonment.

For Ari, awareness seeped in at its own pace—the nearly faded bands of light from the window, the soft sound of forsythia fronds brushing the glass, the faint scent of polished wood and linen, and Cord, beside her, close to her, part of her. Through drugged senses and languid satisfaction the knowledge of what had happened came to her, inarguable. She had made love to Cord Prescott and changed her life.

She murmured something against his ear, words that she knew he couldn't understand, words about love.

He shifted, rubbed his cheek against the side of her hair in a soft caress, then lifted himself on one elbow to raise his weight from her. Her arm tightened around his back, pulling him down, resisting the magnetic compulsion of his gaze—the look that wanted to search out the truth, the meaning of it.

It wasn't a time for meanings. She didn't want meanings. She wanted the strength of his arms and the warmth of his breath against her hair, the strong beat of his heart where she laid her palm flat on his chest, in communication that didn't need words.

In time, he lifted his head to grin at her, sexy, satisfied, masculine. "The spoils of battle," he said, drawling the words. "Wars have been fought over this. You can see why."

She gazed back at him, one eyebrow raised. "How spoiled do you have to be, to be a spoil of battle?"

His lips nuzzled her ear. "How spoiled do you want to be?"

"Oh, quite a bit, I think."

"Do you, now?" He trailed one hand over her breast, his grin now wicked, but the expression faded at her soft sigh. He threaded his hand into her hair and pulled her close, holding her. "You deserve to be spoiled, Arianna. Spoiled and pleas-

ured and . . . all those things . . ." The words
trailed off, replaced by his fingers on the side of
her face, reverent, tender, loving.

She closed her eyes, taking in the wordless caress, supplying the words in her mind she knew he
wouldn't say. His fingers trailed down her neck to
the gold chain and the cameo lying against her
collarbone. "Ari. I wish I could have kept you
from everything in your life that ever hurt you."

His hand cradled her jaw, turning her face
toward him.

She caught his hand in hers, silencing him,
loving him. "No one can do that." She tipped her
face down, rubbing her cheek against his palm.
"When something bad happened to us as children, Pop would cook for us. Cookies. Brownies.
Caramel custard, if it was really bad."

"So how come you don't weigh two hundred
pounds?"

She smiled. "I guess our lives were pretty
good, mostly. My mother didn't like to cook so
much. She would plant a seed, watch something
grow. She grew sunflowers sometimes. They were
my favorites. Most seeds come creeping up, you
can just barely see them. But not sunflowers. They
come up like . . . I don't know. Jack and the
Beanstalk. You can imagine them growing up to
the sky, and being able to climb all the way up,
out of the world."

"Did she plant them after your father was convicted?"

Ari shook her head. "No. Maybe she was afraid we'd just climb up out of the world."

"All of you?"

"My sister and me. No. Just me, I guess. Rosa would have chopped down the stalks because they didn't grow the way she wanted them to. Or where she wanted them to, or something. She was like Pop. Charging into her life, trying to make it do what she wanted it to."

She could feel his smile. "Does it work?"

"Sometimes." She moved her palm against his skin, feeling the smooth resilience of flesh, the bones underneath. "Rosa and Pop can't get along, though. They're too alike. Both wanting to run the world. I don't know what Pop will do if I'm not . . ."

He tightened his arms around her and held her head against his shoulder, fiercely for a moment.

He was about to tell her he wouldn't let her go to jail, she thought. Reassure her with words, promises . . .

She put her fingers against his mouth and stopped him. "Being with you, here, is like that," she said. "I can climb out of the world."

He went quiet for a moment, watchful, examining her, smiling a little as she wove her hands into his hair.

"Don't climb away from me, Ari."

She moved under him, sliding her leg against

his, pleasured as much by the evidence of his response as by her own. "Come with me."

"How high," he muttered in her ear, turning them on their sides, pulling her close to him, "do you want to go?"

She smiled against his skin. "Mm."

"Through the ceiling? To Nita's apartment?"

Her smile widened. She tasted the salt of his skin. "Maybe not that high."

"Yes. We can go right through it. She won't see anything but the gigantic leaves. Can we do that?"

They could. Their bodies knew the way, accommodating to each other's needs the way their minds forged this unlikely emotional bond of two people still held, unreconciled, in the grip of counter purposes. Two people whose lives and values didn't allow for this reckless, mindless sharing, on a disheveled couch, or the sweet reprise of ecstasy.

TEN

In the early-morning darkness Cord's living room was filled with shadows and sensuality, the couch cushions still tumbled on the floor where they'd been left, their clothes strewn haphazardly. Barefoot, wearing an old shirt of Cord's, Ari crossed the room and bent to pick up one of the cushions. She stopped beside the couch, hugging the cushion against her, and sank down on the arm of the sofa, waiting for Cord. He'd stirred and murmured her name when she got out of bed, then reached for her, still half asleep.

She listened to the rasp of his jeans as he pulled them on, and his footsteps across the bedroom. He stopped in the doorway, studying her, then crossed the floor and put his hand on her shoulder.

Leaning into the caress, she let herself absorb the warmth and the strength of his hand for a moment before she spoke. "You told the police we'd be there in the morning," she said, answering the silent question in his gesture. "I didn't know what time you told them. Eight? Seven?"

"I didn't say." His other hand cupped her shoulder, his fingers gentle on the tense muscles. "Are you worried about it?"

"I can't say I'm looking forward to it."

"I'll be there with you. We can go over your statement before you give it. I'll call Oslund. Arrange for him to be there. Then you won't have to say it more than once. He'll know what position we're dealing from—"

"No."

His hands stilled on her shoulders. She could feel his puzzlement, his concern. He was trying to figure her out, she thought. Logically, from a lawyer's point of view. "You don't want Oslund there?" he asked after a moment.

She set the couch cushion down where it belonged, trying to find the words to explain what she wanted. What had changed. "If they ask where I spent the night," she said finally, letting a smile touch her mouth, "I could say I slept on your couch."

"If anyone asks where you spent the night, I won't let you answer. It's none of their business. I'll tell them it's irrelevant."

"I doubt you'll have to. People don't ask such things, usually. They just wonder." She sighed. "But that makes it worse, sometimes, don't you think? Then there's no way to explain your side to them. You can't bring it up. You just have to let them think the worst."

"Ari." The concern in his voice was stronger now, with a touch of wariness. She was worrying him, she thought. She should just come out and say it.

She took in a breath. "I want to go to trial," she said quietly. "I've decided. I don't want to make a deal."

His hands tightened on her shoulders, gripping her hard, startling her. He loosened his hold, then clasped her shoulders again with careful, deliberate pressure. "No," he said, as if he could cancel out her decision with a single syllable.

"Oslund doesn't have to be there," she said, her voice still level. "It will be what you told him. You can see him in court."

"I can see him just as well over a conference table to cut a deal. I know him. I know what I can get from him. What the hell is this about, Arianna?"

She didn't answer him.

He let go of her to walk around in front of her. His chest was bare, his hair unkempt from the times she'd run her hands through it, his eyes dark in the shadowed room but glinting with uneasy reaction to what she was telling him. He put his hands on her shoulders again and pulled her a little closer, demanding her attention, as if, she thought, she was wandering in what she was saying and he would drag her back to focus.

She clasped his wrists. "I don't want to plead guilty to something I didn't do, Cord. I don't want to make a deal. I thought I could. I thought it didn't matter, that kind of . . . lie." Her voice caught. "But it does. I can't do it. I have to tell them the truth, and just hope . . . just hope they believe me."

He clasped the back of her head, holding her, intensity edging his voice. "Listen to me, Arianna. Hoping they believe you isn't good enough. The stakes have been raised on this case. This isn't some slick paper crime anymore. Someone planted a firebomb in that building."

"It wasn't me."

"You can prove that?"

She blinked, studying him for some meaning she hadn't taken in. "But I called in the fire before I went into the building."

"So what? Who's to say you didn't go in there to set the bomb, and it went off before you anticipated? Then you called it in. No witnesses, no one saw you go in. No one to say it wasn't you. You go to trial with this, Arianna, you could go away for a long time."

She stared at him, taking in the bizarre explanation, unbalanced by an aspect of her troubles she hadn't considered. "But that's not what happened. I was just there, by coincidence."

"Yeah," he said, the word clipped. "Like your

father was just by coincidence the one who looked guilty of embezzlement." When she didn't answer him, he went on, "This is the strategy, Arianna. You tell the police the story—simple and direct. You were outside my office. Tell them you were waiting for me. You saw smoke. You called in the fire, and you went in to try to put it out. That's it."

"I wasn't waiting for you. I won't lie."

He let go of her so abruptly, she rocked back on the arm of the couch. "Ari," he said tightly, his patience forced, "if you tell them you were sitting in a car outside my office, trying to decide whether or not to talk to me, the D.A. is going to think you decided it would be more effective to make your point with a bomb."

"How can he prove something I didn't do?"

"He doesn't have to prove it. He just has to drop a few hints, make a few prejudicial insinuations, and every member of the jury will believe it. If you give him the slightest edge on this, Arianna, he could decide to go for blood. We could kiss good-bye any kind of a deal."

She stared at him a long moment. "There was a time when you wanted to go to trial. You were the one to suggest it."

"That was when I thought we had a case, Arianna," he said harshly. "I wanted to win it. I wanted to do what I excel at, dammit. I wanted another notch in my belt."

She flinched at the words, but her voice stayed

calm, riding over her hurt and the anger beneath it. "And now you don't think your chances for another notch are good enough?"

A long span of tension hummed in the room, like the sharpening bands of light from the window, the relentlessly wakening day outside the apartment.

"This isn't about my chances. It's about yours!"

"My chances." She swallowed hard. "My chances for what, I wonder? Confessing to a crime I didn't commit in return for implicating someone else who didn't commit it either?"

"Your chance to stay out of jail, lady. You could go to prison. For years. You think that's nothing to worry about? You think it's something to do to *protect the people you care about,* like some kind of common courtesy? We're talking about prison, Arianna. If you're in danger of forgetting that, ask Pop."

She glared at him, disbelief and shock mixed together in the hot color that flared across her cheeks, in the emotion that shook in her voice. "I don't have to ask. And I don't need to have you tell me what could happen to me, or what it would mean in my life. You think I haven't thought about what's going to happen to me after this? You think I don't have that in my mind all the time—when I'm working, when I'm going to court, when I'm talking about my case, or worrying about Pop, or . . . making love?"

He shut his eyes on the flash of pain she knew he didn't want her to see. His jaw clenched hard enough to define the muscles at the side of his face. "I'll tell you what's going to happen to you, Arianna. You're going to go to the police and give them a statement. You're going to refuse to answer any questions I deem irrelevant or intrusive on your rights. I'm going to get a copy of all the evidence the police have on this firebomb, and I'm going to take it to Oslund and make a deal with him that will keep you out of jail."

"And then what?" Silence clanged down around the words like a prison gate, holding them both immobile, separated by a barrier, she realized, that had no key. "I go back to my work?"

"Yes."

"Where do you think I'm going to get work? You and Charlie will offer me a couple of contracts, pull some strings to keep my business from going under? Make a few deals on my behalf?"

"Yes. That's exactly it."

"Is it? And how far does it go? Bribe a few officials? Give Oslund a couple of cases, to pay him back for going easy on me? Come up with a few false reasons to explain to your colleagues why you're supporting me?"

"I don't give a damn what my colleagues think. I don't give a damn what Oslund thinks. Why the hell should you? What the hell is so sacred about this that you can't lie to Oslund?"

"It's not Oslund. It's Pop. And Victor. And Andy. And . . . you."

He grabbed her again by the shoulders, hard, half shaking her. "I'll tell you what you can do for me, lady. You can stay out of jail. That's what I care about."

"I won't—"

"Won't what? Don't be stupid!"

"I'm not stupid," she said carefully. "But I won't lie. And I didn't—"

"Dammit, I don't care what you did or didn't do!"

She flinched. The room seemed to close in around her, like the dingy walls of a prison cell. Her voice didn't seem to come from her body. She wasn't sure how she made it work, made it sound so normal. "You mean that, don't you? You don't care whether I'm innocent or not."

"Ari . . . for God's sake . . ."

She pulled away from him, struggling for breath, fighting for control with all the fierce resistance she'd learned from the years as her father's daughter. Cord reached for her, but she stepped back, stung by the touch, wounded to the core of her being by the shocking echo of the way he'd touched her all night.

His eyes darkened with a pain she couldn't doubt, but the hard core of his anger, his desperate grasp on the world as he knew it, as he saw it, still held him. "You think it's going to change anything," he asked, "if you go charging into court armed with your innocence and nothing else? You think that's going to save you? That it's going to make one damn bit of difference in the way the system works?"

"I didn't want to save the system," she said. Tears thickened her voice despite the struggle she was waging to keep the tears shut down into one small lump of grief in her chest. "Not the whole system. Just us, Cord."

Heavy, dead silence filled up all the spaces for sound. Finally, defeated by it, she looked down at the floor, where the stripes of light from the window stretched across the floorboards toward the doorway as if searching for an exit.

For Cord, something inside him twisted around a core of emotion so strong, it scared the hell out of him.

What he wanted, despite logic, reason, everything he used to make sense of his life, was to take her back to bed, pull the drapes closed, and make love to her until everything they'd said here was burned away in a heat that didn't allow for words or arguments or thought.

She might have let him. She might have given in to the pressure of his hand on her shoulder, stopped fighting him after a moment and let him pull her back into that seductive, sensual space they'd made together last night. She had strength he couldn't imagine to resist what she thought was wrong, but she had no defenses against her own emotions. She'd given all the defenses to him.

He shut his eyes for a minute and pushed away the slice of pain that went through him like acid.

When he looked at her again, she was watching him with that level gaze, the look steady, vulnerable, unafraid of the truth.

"I'm not salvageable, Ari," he said through gritted teeth. "Don't even try. You won't succeed."

She didn't flinch at the words. She'd steeled herself not to, he thought. She took in his sentence, evaluated it, decided not to contest it. Standing up, she moved away from him, then walked back to the bedroom, carefully stepping around the cushions on the floor.

He heard her picking up her clothes, and behind the partly closed door caught a glimpse of her putting them on, pushing her arm into a sleeve, bending to slip on her jeans. The rasp of the zipper hissed in the dark room.

He didn't try to stop her. Some shred of common sense held out against the mindless frustration that urged him to stalk in after her, slam the bedroom door, and settle their differences any way he could, ethics, logic, common sense be damned.

It wouldn't work, he told himself. It wouldn't change the tough, hard facts that Arianna Rossini was so willing to ignore. The best he could do was to let her go, get some distance between them, and come up with a logical plan of attack for talking to the police later that morning.

She left the bedroom and walked across the living room, unlocked the door, then turned back. He expected a formal, polite good-bye. What he saw instead was the burning, determined flare of her anger. "There are worse things than ending up like Pop, you know," she said. "There's ending up like Charlie." She walked out, closing the door behind her.

The bitter taste in his mouth and the knot in the middle of his chest weren't relevant, Cord argued with himself. The sense of loss so profound it was only a hair's breadth away from rage was controllable.

It had to be, he thought savagely. He had no choice, and neither did she. A couple of hours from now, before she faced the police, she'd have to call him. In the cold, hard light of an impending police interrogation, she'd realize why she couldn't afford to base her life on an emotion as unlitigable as what had held them both last night. She'd realize why she needed him.

That thought kept the hole in his gut from swallowing him up until his phone rang and he picked up the receiver to take the calls from his answering service.

He didn't need to go to the police station this morning, the service told him. Ms. Rossini had called with instructions.

She'd fired him.

The crowd at Eddie's didn't ever change enough for anyone to notice, Cord decided, his elbow on the bar, his attitude as explosive and potentially dangerous as the smack of pool balls in the back room.

Maybe it was the fact that most of the patrons were lawyers.

Or maybe it was him. A lawyer, with a piece missing. Part of his soul. Nothing he could think of would begin to fill up the hole.

"Here. Drink this, for God's sake."

Cord's gaze flicked down to the Scotch that had been set in front of him, then moved, impassively, to the woman who'd perched herself on the stool next to him. "Why?" he asked. "You planning to get me drunk and set me up in a pool game?"

Elaine Andress pulled a face and raised her eyebrows at him. "No. I was hoping it would improve your mood."

"If I thought there was any possibility of that naive hope, I'd drink it. What do you want, Elaine?"

"Nothing," she said, then added, when he slanted her a glance, "Charlie sent me. He's worried about you."

Cord touched the drink Elaine had set down in front of him, rubbing his fingertips along the cold, wet rim of the glass, turning it in place, leaving it where it was. "I've known Charlie most of my life, Elaine. And you know, I've been wondering lately what he worries over."

"You should be telling him about it, not me," Elaine said. "You need to mend some fences there. He thinks you're on some kind of damn crusade. And you know what I think?"

"I have a feeling I'm about to find out."

"I think he's right."

He smiled without humor. "You're on his side of the fence, are you?" he asked in a tone of voice intended to defuse Elaine's irrepressible curiosity.

She stared at him long enough to let him know she wasn't defused. "It's not your case anymore, Cord."

He felt his jaw clench. Carefully, consciously, he made himself let go of the tangled knot of emotions that tightened whenever he thought of Ari. "I'm aware of that."

"She's got another lawyer, Cord. He's not Kent and Prescott, but he's good enough."

"I know that."

She didn't ask him how he knew it. Cord's continuing interest—no, obsession—with a case that was no longer his didn't fall within the parameters of appropriate.

"Dammit," she said. "Charlie's *sorry!* He's worried about you. He probably wishes he'd just shredded the damn invoices before anyone had seen them!"

"What are you talking about?"

"Charlie was the one the auditors called first,

Cord. He owns the building, after all. He was the one who had to explain what she must have been doing. He didn't want to. Can't you cut him a little slack?"

Cord's hand tightened around his Scotch glass until the knuckles were white. "Charlie's the one who implicated her?"

Elaine shrugged. "She was already implicated, Cord. She was the logical suspect. What choice did Charlie have but to agree with that? It doesn't mean he didn't feel badly about it."

"Sure thing, Elaine," Cord muttered, his voice low, but with an edge that made her frown at him. "My partner feels badly about his part in indicting an innocent woman. Why can't I cut him a little slack? Give him a little sympathy, is that it?"

Elaine set her drink down on the bar and turned toward him, her eyes widening in uncharacteristic surprise. "You're in love with her, aren't you?"

The words of protest, the suave, worldly denial, crowded to the front of his mind, ready to come out, ready to squelch the always-eager component of rumor that spiced Elaine's stories. The words evaporated, though, thinned and disappeared beneath the sharp, knife-hard edge of his reaction to her statement.

"No comment," he managed to say, staring into the drink that couldn't help him.

Too late, he realized what that hole in his gut meant.

It meant he wasn't going to win this case, no matter what precedents he invoked, what arguments he mustered, what kind of pain caught his chest at odd moments and robbed him of the ability to breathe. *In love with her* didn't cut it. What Ari had asked of him went beyond the ragged and damaged notion he held of love. She wanted idealism. Faith. Trust. Pieces of himself he'd lost too long ago to retrieve.

Arianna Rossini had finally seen what he was, and made the decision she should have made the first time she met him.

The only thing he could do for her now was to leave her alone.

What he could do for himself he couldn't imagine.

Tomas Rossini walked into Cord's office without an appointment, belligerent and stubborn and expecting to be refused.

Cord let him in right away.

As he poured a cup of coffee and handed it across the desk, he studied the older man's hunched shoulders and jutting chin, waiting for him to speak.

Tomas took the coffee, finally, and sat down, but he said, "I didn't come to drink coffee. I've been to see my daughter's new lawyer."

Cord didn't respond. Tomas wrapped his cup

in both his hands and met Cord's eyes with his own stubborn glare.

"This new lawyer—he wants me to go on the stand, to testify, when my daughter's trial comes. He thinks I can help. He's not so happy about how the trial might turn out."

Cord shut his eyes for just a second, closing out a flash of pain too private to share. When he opened them again, however, the faint lift of the older man's eyebrows indicated he'd seen it.

"Is that why you didn't want to take my daughter's case to trial?" he demanded. "Is that why she fired you? You thought you would lose?"

"I didn't want to take the risk," Cord said, "but that's not why she fired me. There were . . . personal reasons. Hers. It was what she wanted. I had to respect that choice. I owed her that."

Ari's father reached out and set the coffee cup on the desk, as if he were giving it back, or refusing to take it in the first place. "My daughter is a grown woman. Strong, smart. But she has only loved two men in her life. Both of them hurt her."

Cord didn't pretend not to understand. His hands curled into fists on the desk, and there was a muscle in the side of his face so tight, it made his jaw ache.

"How is she?"

The older man's frown was fierce, but as he looked at Cord, glancing down to the clenched fists, the tension in his shoulders, the anger faded into something else. "Not eating," he said. "Not sleeping. I hear her up at all hours, walking around. I find her with blueprints out on the table, claiming she's working. She broke the chain to her mother's necklace because she was holding on to it so hard."

Cord covered his eyes with one hand, pressing his fingers into his temples.

"She wouldn't let me get it fixed for her," Tomas went on. "She didn't want to part with it, she said. I gave it to her mother before Arianna was born. My wife wore it every day when I was in prison. She never doubted me. She never stopped being loyal to me."

Cord Prescott made a sound that would have been lost in a room where the silence wasn't so heavy. It didn't have any words, but it carried enough meaning to make Tomas frown at the man who'd made it, reassessing him.

He spread his gnarled hands on his knees, leaning forward, lifting his chin. "Your partner came to my house a week ago," he said.

"I know."

"He was full of advice to my daughter, expecting me to back him up. He told her when you play soccer, you don't think about your teammates. You don't worry about being loyal. You just worry about winning. But he was wrong. It was never like that when we played soccer. We were a team. We helped each other. That was why I went to him when I needed a lawyer. I didn't know how much people could change." He pinned Cord with a steady, challenging look. "I was wrong about him. Sometimes I'm wrong about people."

"Not often, I'd bet."

"Maybe I was wrong about you. I don't know."

"You thought I was going to hurt Ari. You weren't wrong."

"Am I wrong now?"

Cord had no answer.

In the fading afternoon light, the air in the office seemed dense with expectation and undecided possibilities.

"About what?" Cord asked finally.

Tomas placed his palms flat on the desk and lifted himself out of the chair, then he leaned toward Cord, getting a good look at him across the desk, making sure he was looking back. "You told me you'd keep my daughter out of jail."

"Yes."

"Now I want you to do it."

ELEVEN

"All rise."

Two dozen occupants of the courtroom obeyed the bailiff's order. Arianna stood between her father and her lawyer, John Ferris, a young man she'd hired on the recommendation of her sister. Charlie had called and offered, again, to represent her. She'd refused. She hadn't even wanted to speak to him. All the emotional connections with Cord were still too ragged for her to think about without pain. When she'd told Pop, the morning after she'd spent the night with Cord, that he wouldn't be representing her after all, her throat had been so tight, she'd barely been able to get the words out. She'd had to wave off his questions and walk out of the house to keep from breaking down in front of him.

"Be seated."

The shuffling of feet was hollow with the echoes of ghosts, crowding into the empty seats that had been filled at her arraignment with defendants, lawyers, distraught families. Inside her, she felt the same fear she'd felt that day; it expanded every time she took a breath, settled back when she breathed out, but not enough. She tried to center herself as she had then, finding what she needed to say, what she needed to do.

It was a mistake. The memories of Cord were too close, too vivid. His assurance, his steady, solid presence beside her, the core of sensitivity she'd sensed was there before he let her see it. And the other memories. Outside on the lawn, in his office, at his apartment.

Tears stung the corners of her eyes, threatening again, as they had so often in the past two weeks. She needed him, needed the thought of him, yet it brought as much pain as help—an empty ache where she missed him, a hole in her heart that should have been filled with something he'd refused to give to her. Or to himself.

That was the sharpest knowledge, the center of her pain. Cord didn't believe she was guilty. She knew that. But he'd never been able to tell her so. It would have meant rejecting that part of himself he'd come to think of as real—the part that didn't believe in trust, or innocence, or love.

She'd thought, for one night, that maybe he could start believing, that maybe there was some chance . . .

Pop's hand touched her arm. The others were

already sitting. The judge stared at her in mild surprise, her lawyer cleared his throat. Ari sat down, feeling the chill in her body that came with the sudden return of her surroundings.

Pop squeezed her hand, reassuring her, but she could feel the tremors under the reassurance. A trickle of worry for him added itself to the turmoil of emotions inside her.

She hadn't wanted him to come. He'd taken her hand when she was arguing with him and turned it over, looking at it, her short-clipped nails, the carpenter's creases in her palm.

"I didn't let my family come to my trial," he'd said. "I thought I was protecting them. I thought I was the strong one. I wondered, afterward, sometimes—when your mother was home waiting to hear, did she think, 'I'll let him believe he's protecting me. He needs to think he's strong'?"

Ari hadn't answered him. Her throat had been too tight. But they both knew she wouldn't make him stay away.

John Ferris was standing now, speaking, presenting a motion to the court. He'd explained it to her. It had some Latin phrase to describe what it was supposed to be, a request for more time, a delay before they had to go to trial, but to her it had sounded desperate and farfetched. She couldn't believe it would work. And just as she'd thought, the judge was shaking his head, saying something dismissive.

Her lawyer came back to sit down at the defense table, turned to her, and murmured, "We're going on with the jury selection."

She nodded. *The jury. Her peers, who would judge her.*

The potential jurors were seated at the back of the room, waiting to be called. At the first name, she made herself turn around to see the face of the person coming forward. A woman, middle-aged, slight, well dressed. Then a man, young, skeptical, glancing at her as if she were an exhibit in a museum.

Her panic rose when he looked away, expanding into a catch in her breathing. *He didn't believe she was innocent.* The image of Cord standing in his living room, shirtless, his hair still disheveled from the times they'd made love, telling her he didn't care whether she'd done this, rose in her mind.

She wanted him here. She wanted him here.

Her father put his hand on her shoulder, steadying her. Her lawyer was saying, "Ms. Rossini . . . ?"

"Yes?"

"Are you all right?"

"Yes. Thank you." She felt as if she were turning numb from the inside out, first her soul, then her heart. Her body would follow. She clung to sensation, the grain of the wood at the worn edge of her chair, the cool draft from the anteroom when the door opened and closed, the smell of stale coffee.

There was movement at the back of the room, someone coming in, a murmur of voices and a sharp look from the judge. She turned to follow his gaze. With her heart suddenly beating too fast, his name like an unexpected taste on her tongue, she gripped the back of the chair and stared.

Gray eyes stared back at her, solemn, serious in a way that didn't seem connected to the unreality of seeing him there, as if she'd called him up from her imagination.

She must have made some sound. Her father's arm came around her shoulders. There was a buzz of speculation, heads turning, expectations focused on Cord as he walked toward the front of the room. He stopped beside her, staring at her while she searched desperately for words she was afraid to speak.

"Ari . . ." he said finally.

The judge banged the gavel, demanding attention. Cord tore his gaze away from her and walked toward the bench.

"Your honor," he said, his voice steady, sounding prosaically normal against the background of still-buzzing reaction. "I have evidence pertinent to the disposition of this trial."

"Your honor!" Oslund protested.

Cord wasn't looking at him. He was looking, again, at Ari, his eyes carrying a message she couldn't read over the hammering of her heart. *What was he doing there?*

The gavel banged. "Mr. Prescott," the judge

stated, "my understanding is that you are no longer counsel to the defendant in this case."

Cord faced the bench. "That's correct."

"What, then, are you doing here?" the judge asked, eyebrows raised.

"I'm here to enter a guilty plea."

"The plea has already been entered, Mr. Prescott. You were here when it was. I trust you recall the—"

"—The circumstances have changed."

"Your honor, I object!" Oslund stood up and took a step toward Cord.

"I can understand why you might," the judge said dryly.

For Cord, Oslund might not have existed. He looked back at Ari and she felt a wave of heat and then cold sweep over her, making her dizzy, as if the time that had passed since that morning and now were dissolving between them.

When he turned back to the judge his words were quiet, but she heard them distinctly. "This woman is not guilty."

"You can consult with defense and present your evidence at the trial, Mr. Prescott—assuming the defendant wants you to."

"Whether she wants me to or not, this trial should not take place," Cord said.

The judge's lined, jowled face was almost comical in its incredulity. "Mr. Prescott, you are an attorney. I presume you still remember the protocol of a courtroom. I've heard enough of this—"

"I plead guilty to this crime," Cord snapped as the bailiff moved toward him.

". . . What?"

"On behalf of the firm of Kent and Prescott."

The murmuring in the courtroom rose to a confused buzz. Around her, Ari was aware of people shifting in their seats, shocked voices. She stared at Cord as if nothing was happening around them, as if she were the only witness to this act.

The gavel banged repeatedly, finally quieting the room. "Mr. Prescott," the judge said into the near silence, "you may consult with the . . . present defense counsel, and then, presumably, take up your case with the district attorney. This court will reconvene tomorrow at ten o'clock. I think we've covered enough ground here today to satisfy everyone."

Cord turned toward her. His gaze found hers without taking in anything else in the room, as if there were nothing between them—no court-room, no witnesses to this meeting, no days and nights of longing and loneliness. She stood and moved away from her seat, taking steps toward him. She stopped just before they touched, uncertain. Then she reached for him and was locked in his arms, wrapped in an embrace she clung to as tightly as he did.

"It's over, Ari," he said softly, against her ear.

"It will be dismissed tomorrow. I promise that. It's done for you."

Surrounded by the ebb and flow of the courtroom spectators, they held each other close, gripping hard, desperate for the contact.

She took in the shape of his body against hers, his warmth, the sound of his voice, as if she were starving and he was food and water, but she couldn't quite let herself believe it was for her.

"It's over," he said again. "No one—*no one* can convict you once I tell them what I've learned."

"But what—?"

"I don't know if I can prove it. I don't have all the evidence yet. I might be implicated myself. I was his partner . . ."

"Charlie?"

"Yes. Charlie." He swallowed. "My partner. Charlie."

He moved his head, released her a little, and said, "Yes, Pop. It was Charlie."

Behind her, her father muttered, "Charlie?"

Cord let go of her with one hand, turning her with his arm around her shoulders to face Pop.

"I should have seen it earlier," Cord said, "but I didn't. Not until your father came to see me. It was something he said about teamwork, and about how people change. It wasn't hard to put it together after that. Charlie's always needed money. He planted those invoices in your desk, before the investigators arrived. He'd been collecting money on the grant, forging your signature. It wasn't hard. He had access to it whenever he wanted it. And he'd done this before. He'd done it in your father's case." He glanced again toward Pop. "I intend to bring that up too. It'll be public knowledge—your innocence."

Pop's hands gripped the edges of his jacket as if he didn't know what else to do with them. His eyes were still baffled, but his mouth had stretched into a tentative smile.

"You went to see Cord, Pop?" Ari said.

The older man nodded. "But I guess you've gone further than keeping my daughter out of jail, lawyer."

"Oh, yes. I've gone further. And I want to go way beyond that, Pop." Cord looked at Ari again, and his voice dropped to a low murmur that was rough with emotion. "I want to prove I'm not Charlie."

"Oh, Cord, you don't—"

"Yes." He silenced her with a finger on her lips. "I do. That's where I was headed, babe. Maybe I was starting on that long slide down, but I got lucky. I walked into a jail cell and met something that stopped me. Someone. And if you'll give me another chance . . ."

She was in his arms before he finished, holding him, her cheek pressed against his shoulder. She heard his long sigh, felt his breath on her hair, his arms clamped so tightly around her back, she couldn't breathe.

She didn't need to breathe. Heedless of the

courtroom, the curious stares of the remaining spectators, Oslund's hovering presence, she let him kiss her. She kissed him back, murmured words against his mouth that she didn't bother to understand, and felt his heartbeat in counterpoint to her own.

The strangers around them could have been guests they'd gathered to witness their joining, the officers of the court could have been seal and symbol of their commitment. Reckless, smiling, untouched even by Oslund's scowl, Ari linked her hands behind Cord's neck and let her gaze linger on his face, his smile, the leap of joy in his eyes.

His thumbs stroked her eyebrows, the corners of her eyes, her cheeks, the tucks at the edge of her smile. His own mouth widened, smiling, smiling.

"What?" she said.

"You. I need you, Ari. I need you."

Her smile crumbled as she caught her lip between her teeth. "I need you too. I've missed you so much."

His hands framed her face. "I never doubted your innocence in my heart, Ari. From the moment I saw you I knew. I knew the truth."

"So did I. I love you." It was a whisper, a breath, words spoken too softly for anyone else to hear. Caught in it, they both stilled, unmoving, lost in the promise.

Oslund took a few steps toward them, cleared

his throat, and muttered, his voice rusty, "Prescott."

Distracted, Cord glanced toward him, then back to Ari. "I think I'm about to be arrested," he said, then, incongruously, smiled.

She grinned back at him, giddy, laughing for no reason that made any sense. "I think you are."

"Come on, Prescott," Oslund said. "You've got some questions to answer."

"Will you bail me out?" he asked her.

Laughing again, set off by the pointless question as if they were drugged, they clung to each other. "Yes," she got out through her strained throat. "I'll bail you out."

Oslund put his hand on Cord's shoulder, heavy and peremptory. Slowly, by degrees, Cord loosened his hold on her, let her go. He glanced toward Oslund, but then lifted her face to his and kissed her again, lingering, tender, slow enough to give her his heart in it. When he released her, he moved his mouth to her ear and whispered, "I love you."

It was enough. Enough, as Cord turned toward the district attorney and took a breath to face the necessary questions, as Ari let her father's arm support her and comfort her as he walked her back to her own attorney, waiting patiently to tell them the formal details of what would happen.

It would be enough, she decided, to hang their lives on.

Watching Cord across the room as he glanced

over at her, she knew that. There would be a trial.
Cord would prove Charlie guilty. Or not. Either
way, there would be pain, loss, anguish.

But she loved him, and he loved her back.

That truth would be the light they moved
toward, inevitably, surely, without falter.

It would be enough.

Pop put his hand on her shoulder again. She
covered it with her own and turned toward him,
realizing his hand was trembling, his eyes were
bright with tears.

"Pop. Here. Sit down."

"No."

"We'll both sit down, Pop. Here." They sat
together on the hard chairs, hands clasped.

"Pop," she said again, her voice hoarse from
the lump of emotion in her throat, "I don't know
what to say. Thank you for going to Cord. Thank
you for being with me. For always loving me."

"Ach." He turned toward her, his smile
crooked. "I shouldn't go to my future son-in-law
and ask a favor? We should have had a lawyer in
the family a long time ago, I guess."

"I don't know that he's your future son-in-law,
Pop. He hasn't—"

"Hasn't asked you?" He frowned. "Why not?"

She smiled and let out a huff of laughter.
"Give him a minute, Pop. He's busy being arrested."

EPILOGUE

Cord banged in another nail, three straight strokes. The head sank into the wood, true and level, neat enough to satisfy even Pop.

Cord sat back on his heels and grinned. He'd outraged his father-in-law by telling him banging nails was just like shooting pool, when in Pop's mind carpentry was clearly a higher art form. Pop had considered it his duty to teach his son-in-law how to hammer in a straight nail. He wanted to make sure his grandchildren would be brought up right.

It had been clear, at first, that he'd had some doubts about Cord Prescott as his daughter's husband. For months Cord and Pop had been awkward with each other, Pop aloof, prickly about their differing social backgrounds, Cord overly courteous, and both of them too aware that Pop's gruff antagonism was tempered only because his daughter wished it.

Halfway through Charlie's trial, when Ari had been asked to testify and had agreed to do it, Tomas had quarreled with her and lost the argument. He'd showed up at Cord's office, disgruntled and put out with his daughter, and helped himself with very little invitation to Cord's brandy. "Don't have daughters," he'd muttered. "You can't teach them anything."

After the second brandy he'd asked about Cord's father, and listened to his son-in-law's words with quiet attentiveness that had led Cord to say more than he'd intended.

"Your father was a good lawyer," Tomas had said much later. "He taught you the best of what he knew, I guess." Then, quietly, "Maybe some of your children will be lawyers. I could have a granddaughter who's a lawyer, you think? Maybe it wouldn't be such a bad thing."

"I'll see what I can do about it," he'd said, and Pop had laughed and, unexpectedly, winked at him.

"You do that," he'd said.

Cord gradually realized that at the silence of his own hammer the sounds in the other room had stopped too. He looked toward the doorway just as Ari appeared there, grinning at him, a smudge of sawdust across her cheek, holding a soda in each hand.

"I can't hammer another nail without a break," he told her. "Come over here."

He took both of the cans from her and set them on the plywood subfloor, then grasped her hands and pulled her down in front of him. He settled her on the floor between his legs, her back to his chest, where he could wrap his arms around her and rest his chin on the top of her head. Against her stomach he made slow, sensual circles with his hands, riding a little higher with each pass until he covered her breasts with his palms.

She tipped her head back against his shoulder, and he could see the edge of her slow, teasing smile. "Is this what you think about when you should be hammering?"

He smiled back. "Let's buy a forty-five-foot boat and sail around the world."

"I have to get better at sailing first."

"You will. You have the knack. And you like it."

She laughed. "That's what you were thinking?"

"No. I was thinking we should have a couple of daughters. They could grow up and become carpenters and take over the job for me."

"Or they could become lawyers and need more office space and you'd be hammering nails forever."

"Your father once suggested that."

"Not lately, I'll bet."

"No. Not lately." Pop had been outraged to

hear that Charlie Kent was appealing his guilty verdict, and was free of consequences until the appeal was heard. *You get another chance, Pop. That's the law*, Cord had told him.

And sometimes in life too, he thought. The odd, stray gift of chance. Like the application he'd happened to glance at on his secretary's desk at the top of the "To be filed" box. He hadn't been looking for an assistant, but the name had caught his eye. Minh. A young woman, a law student commuting to Suffolk University from Worcester. The address had been in one of the city's poorer sections, not far from the convenience store where the murder had taken place. Cord had canceled his afternoon's appointments, put on his coat, and gone there. He'd hired her on the spot and had had no cause to regret it. Susan Minh was hardworking, efficient, intelligent, and good-natured about sharing temporary office space with his secretary in the rented quarters Cord had moved to when he'd sold the office he'd owned jointly with Charlie.

In the new building Susan would have her own office. There wouldn't be long to wait. Ari's crew was finishing it with a speed that to Cord seemed nothing short of miraculous. He'd come here this Sunday afternoon more to admire his wife's accomplishment than to work.

He smiled down at her, then shifted around a little so that he could kiss the corner of her mouth. "How about it?" he murmured. "A daughter?"

"What if she becomes a lawyer?"

He moved his hands to her throat and unfastened the top button of her shirt. "She can bail me out next time I'm in jail."

"You haven't been in jail."

"But I've been arrested."

"You weren't really arrested. You were just questioned. Detained."

He grinned at her. "That's a lawyer's distinction, don't you think? You're developing a legal mind, Arianna."

"Deliver me," she said, smiling.

Leaning back, he pulled her on top of him, stretched out full-length on the new floor. "Maybe I can arrange that."

"What did you have in mind, Counselor?"

He got her shirt off and bunched it up under his head for a pillow. "A discovery motion, I think," he murmured. "If it pleases the court."

He heard the smile in her voice as he stroked the smooth valley of her spine, stopping at the clasp of her bra. "Never mind the court. Just please the client."

He pleased both of them.

Later, lying amidst their strewn clothes, absorbing the smell of new wood and the spacious luxury of empty rooms—the shape and promise of new construction, of building their lives the way they would build this structure—he mused, half amused and marveling at the thought, that he would plant a tree by the front entrance.

They'd tend it together with faith, hope, and love.

THE EDITOR'S CORNER

Along with May flowers come four terrific new LOVESWEPTs that will dazzle you with humor, excitement, and passion. Reading the best romances from the finest authors—what better way to enjoy the beauty and magic of spring?

Starting things off is the fabulous Mary Kay McComas with a love story that is the **TALK OF THE TOWN**, LOVESWEPT #738. Rosemary Wickum always finds some wonderful treasures in the refuse center, pieces perfect for her metal sculptures, but one thing she never goes looking for is a man! When recycling whiz Gary Albright begins pursuing her with shameless persistence, everyone in town starts rooting for romance. Once he nurses the embers of her passion back to life, he must convince his lady he'll always warm her heart. Irresistible characters and frisky humor make this latest Mary Kay story a tenderhearted treat—and proves that love can find us in the most unlikely places.

From the delightful Elaine Lakso comes another winner with **TASTING TROUBLE**, LOVE-SWEPT #739. Joshua Farrington doesn't think much of the Lakeview Restaurant's food or ambience, but its owner Liss Harding whets his interest and provokes him into a brash charade! Tempting her with strawberries, kissing her in the wine cellar, Josh coaxes her to renovate the building, update the menu —and lose herself in his arms. But once he confesses his identity, he has to persuade her he isn't the enemy. As delectable as chocolate, as intoxicating as fine wine, this wonderful romance from Elaine introduces charming, complex lovers whose dreams are more alike than they can imagine.

From the ever-popular Erica Spindler comes **SLOW HEAT**, LOVESWEPT #740. Jack Jacobs thrives on excitement, thrills to a challenge, and always plays to win, so when the sexy TV film critic is teamed with Jill Lansing, he expects fireworks! Five years before, they'd been wildly, recklessly in love, but he couldn't give her the promise she'd craved. Now she needs a hero, a man who'll share his soul at last. He is her destiny, her perfect partner in work and in bed, but can Jill make him understand he has to fight for what he wants—and that her love is worth fighting for? Steamy with innuendo, sparkling with wit, Erica's exhilarating battle of the sexes reunites a fiery pair of lovers—and casts an enchanting spell!

Rising star Maris Soule offers a hero who is full of **DARK TEMPTATION**, LOVESWEPT #741. Did special-effects genius Jason McLain really murder his wife, as the tabloids claimed? Valerie Wiggins approaches his spooky old house, hoping to convince him to help her make their Halloween charity event truly frightening. But when he opens the door, her heart races not with fright but sizzling arousal. Jason fears caring for Val will put her in danger, but maybe helping her face her demons will silence his own. Torn by doubts, burning with desire, can a man and a woman who'd first touched in darkness find themselves healed by the dawn? In a heartstopping novel of passion and suspense, Maris explores our deepest terrors and most poignant longings in the journey that transforms strangers into soulmates.

Happy reading!

With warmest wishes,

Beth de Guzman
Senior Editor

Shauna Summers
Associate Editor

P.S. Don't miss the women's novels coming your way in May: **DARK RIDER** from *The New York Times* bestselling author Iris Johansen is an electrifying tale of deadly and forbidden desire that sweeps from the exotic islands of a tropical paradise to the magnificent estates of Regency England; **LOVE STORM** by Susan Johnson, the bestselling mistress of the erotic historical romance, is the legendary, long out-of-print novel of tempestuous passion; **PROMISE ME MAGIC** by the extraordinary Patricia Camden is a "Once Upon a Time" historical romance of passion and adventure in the tradition of Laura Kinsale. And immediately following this page, look for a preview of the exciting romances from Bantam that are *available now!*

Don't miss these extraordinary books
by your favorite Bantam authors

On sale in March:

MISTRESS
by Amanda Quick

DANGEROUS TO KISS
by Elizabeth Thornton

LONG NIGHT MOON
by Theresa Weir

DANGEROUS TO KISS
by Elizabeth Thornton

"A major, major talent . . . a genre superstar."
—*Rave Reviews*

Handsome, kind, and unassuming, Mr. Gray seemed the answer to Deborah Weyman's prayers. For once she accepted the position he offered, she would finally be safe from the notorious Lord Kendal, a man she had good reason to believe had murdered her former employer—and was now after her. But there were certain things about Mr. Gray that Deborah should have noticed: the breadth of his shoulders, the steel in his voice, the gleam in his uncommonly blue eyes—things that might have warned her that Mr. Gray was no savior but a very dangerous man. . . .

"Study hall," said Deborah brightly, addressing Mr. Gray, and all the girls groaned.

With a few muttered protests and a great deal of snickering, the girls began to file out of the room. Deborah assisted their progress by holding the door for them, reminding them cheerfully that on the morrow they would be reviewing irregular French verbs and she expected them to have mastered their conjugations. As the last girl slipped by her, Deborah shut the door with a snap, then rested her back against it, taking a moment or two to collect herself.

Suddenly aware that Mr. Gray had risen at their exit and was standing awkwardly by the window, she politely invited him to be seated. "You'll have a glass of sherry?" she inquired. At Miss Hare's, the guests were invariably treated to a glass of sherry when the ordeal of taking tea was over. At his nod, Deborah moved to the sideboard against the wall. The glasses and decanter were concealed behind a locked door, and she had to stoop to retrieve them from their hiding place.

As he seated himself, Gray's gaze wandered over the lush curves of her bottom. There was an appreciative glint in his eye. The thought that was going through his head was that Deborah Weyman bore no resemblance to the descriptions he had been given of her. Spinsterish? Straitlaced? Dull and uninteresting? That's what she wanted people to think. She had certainly dressed for the part with her high-necked, long-sleeved blue kerseymere and the ubiquitous white mobcap pulled down to cover her hair. An untrained eye would look no further. Unhappily for the lady, not only was he a trained observer, but he was also an acknowledged connoisseur of women. Advantage to him.

Since her attention was riveted on the two glasses of sherry on the tray she was carrying, he took the liberty of studying her at leisure. Her complexion was tinged with gray—powder, he presumed—in an attempt to add years and dignity to sculpted bones that accredited beauties of the *ton* would kill for. The shapeless gown served her no better than the gray face powder. She had the kind of figure that would look good in the current high-waisted diaphanous gauzes or in sackcloth and ashes. Soft, curvaceous, womanly. When she handed him his sherry, he kept his expression blank. Behind the wire-rimmed spectacles, her lustrous green eyes were framed by— he blinked and looked again. Damned if she had not snipped at her eyelashes to shorten them! Had the woman no vanity?

"I missed something, didn't I?" said Deborah. "That's why you are smiling that secret smile to yourself."

"Beg pardon?" Gray's thick veil of lashes lowered to diffuse the intentness of her look.

Deborah seated herself. "I missed something when Millicent offered you a cucumber sandwich. What was it?"

If he had the dressing of her, the first thing he would do was banish the mobcap. There wasn't a curl or stray tendril of hair to be seen. "A note."

"A note?"

"Mmm." Red hair or blond. It had to be one or the other. Unless she had dyed it, of course. He wouldn't put it past her. If this were a tavern and she were not a lady, he would offer her fifty, no, a hundred gold guineas if only she would remove that blasted cap.

"Are you saying that Millicent passed you a note?"

Her voice had returned to its prim and proper mode. He was beginning to understand why she had kept out of the public eye. She couldn't sustain a part.

"The note," Deborah reminded him gently.

"The note? Ah, yes, the note. It was in the cucumber sandwich." She was trying to suppress a smile, and her dimples fascinated him. No one had mentioned that she had dimples.

"Oh dear, I suppose I should show it to Miss Hare. That girl is incorrigible."

"I'm afraid that won't be possible."

"Why won't it?"

"On her way out, she snatched it back. I believe she ate it."

When she laughed, he relaxed against the back of his chair, well pleased with himself. That wary, watchful look that had hovered at the back of her eyes had completely dissipated. He was beginning to take her measure. The more he erased his masculinity, the more trustful she became. Unhappily for him, there was something about Deborah Weyman that stirred the softer side of his nature. Advantage to her.

Deborah sipped at her sherry, trying to contain her impatience. As her prospective employer, it was up to him to begin the interview. He lacked the social graces. She wasn't finding fault with him. On the contrary, his inexperience appealed to her. It made him seem awkward, boyish, harmless. Besides, she had enough social graces for the two of them.

"Miss Hare mentioned that you were seeking a governess for your young sister?" she said.

He was reluctant to get down to business. All too soon, things would change. That trustful look would be gone from her eyes, and Miss Weyman would never trust him again. Pity, but that was almost inevitable. Still, he wasn't going to make things difficult for her at this stage of the game. That would come later.

Deborah shifted restlessly. "You will wish to know

about references from former employers," she said, trying to lead him gently.

"References?" He relaxed a little more comfortably against the back of his chair. Smiling crookedly, he said, "Oh, Miss Hare explained your circumstances to me. Having resided in Ireland with your late husband for a goodly number of years, you allowed your acquaintance with former employers to lapse."

"That is correct."

"I quite understand. Besides, Miss Hare's recommendation carries more weight with me."

"Thank you." She'd got over the first hurdle. Really, it was as easy as taking sweetmeats from a babe. Mr. Gray was more gullible than she could have hoped. The thought shamed her, and her eyes slid away from his.

"Forgive me for asking," he said, "Miss Hare did not make this clear to me. She mentioned that in addition to teaching my sister the correct forms and addresses, you would also impart a little gloss. How do you propose to do that?"

There was an awkward pause, then Mr. Gray brought his glass to his lips and Deborah shrank involuntarily. She knew that she looked like the last person on earth who could impart gloss to anyone.

For a long, introspective moment, she stared at her clasped hands. Seeing that look, Gray asked quietly, "What is it? What have I said?" and leaning over, he drew one finger lightly across her wrist.

The touch of his finger on her bare skin sent a shock of awareness to all the pulse points in her body. She trembled, stammered, then fell silent. When she raised her eyes to his, she had herself well in hand. "I know what you are thinking," she said.

"Do you? I doubt it." He, too, had felt the shock of awareness as bare skin slid over bare skin. The pull on his senses astonished him.

His eyes were as soft as his smile. Disregarding both, she said earnestly, "You must understand, Mr. Gray, that governesses and schoolteachers are not paid to be fashionable. Indeed, employers have a decided preference for governesses who know their place. Servants wear livery. We governesses wear a livery of sorts, too. Well, you must have noticed that the schoolteachers at Miss Hare's are almost indistinguishable, one from the other."

"You are mistaken. I would know you anywhere."

LONG NIGHT MOON

by the spectacular

Theresa Weir

"Theresa Weir's writing is poignant, passionate and powerful . . . will capture the hearts of readers."
—*New York Times* bestselling author Jayne Ann Krentz

With her rare insight into the human heart, Theresa Weir creates tender, emotionally compelling, powerfully satsifying love stories. Now the author whom Romantic Times *praises as "a fresh and electrifying voice in romantic fiction," offers LONG NIGHT MOON, a novel that touches on the nationally important issue of domestic violence and affirms the power of love to heal the deepest sorrows.*

"I don't know what the hell—" His voice caught.

She was lying on her side, facing the window, clasped hands under her head, knees drawn up, eyes open wide, staring at nothing. And she was crying. Without making a sound.

Oh, Christ.

He was a man with no heart, no conscience, but suddenly he ached with an ache that was unbearable.

An ache that tightened his throat and stung his eyes. An ache he remembered but had never wanted to experience again.

For once in his life, he was at a total loss. He didn't speak. He didn't know what to say.

She pulled in a trembling breath. The sound seemed to fill the quiet of the room, adding weight to the ache in his chest. And then she spoke. Quietly, emotionlessly, her very lack of feeling a reflection of her measured control, of words doled out with utmost care.

"I thought I could be somebody else. At least for a little while."

He had no idea what to do, but he found himself pulling her into his arms. He held her, and he rocked her. He breathed in the scent of her. He stroked her hair, letting the satin tresses slide through his fingers.

Instinctively he knew that this was the real Sara Ivy. Not the socialite with her expensive gowns and jewels, not the hard woman who had snubbed him.

And the woman on the beach—she, too, was Sara Ivy. Defiant. Brave. Sexy.

That one drove him crazy.

But this one . . . this one broke his heart.

Time passed. The clock on the desk made its old familiar grinding sound.

Nine o'clock.

Sara lifted her head from his shoulder and let out a sigh. "I have to go."

Feeling strangely fragile, he let her slip out of his arms. Her body left a warm, invisible imprint on him.

She stood, gripping the blanket under her chin. "Don't watch me dress."

He had seen her naked body. He had a photo he stared at almost daily, a photo he'd lied to her about.

He turned. He walked toward the windows. With one finger, he pushed at the blinds. Metal popped, bent, making a triangle he could look through.

The full December moon. Low in the sky, blurry, as if a storm was moving in.

"Don't go," he said quietly, without turning around.

"I have to."

"Why?" He didn't want to think about her going back to Ivy.

She didn't say anything.

He made it a point to avoid intimate conversations, but suddenly he wanted her to talk to him, wanted her to explain things.

Rather than suffer the intrusive glare of a sixty-watt bulb, he opened the blinds, letting in just the right amount of light.

Behind him, he heard her move, heard the soft whisper of her shoes as she crossed the room.

He turned.

She was dressed and slipping into her coat. Her clothes seemed to have given her strength. Some of that cool, aloof control was back.

She went to the phone and called for a cab.

Anger—or was it fear—leaped in him. "What happens if you get home late?" he asked, his voice bordering on sarcasm. "Does he cut off your allowance?"

She silently considered him.

For the last several years, he'd prided himself on

the fact that he knew more about life than anybody. It was an arrogant assumption. Suddenly that truth was never more apparent. As she stared at him, the foundation of his self-assurance wobbled, and he experience a moment of doubt.

He had a sudden image of himself, standing next to a yawning precipice, ready to tumble headlong.

"Yes," she said with a smile that hinted at self-mockery.

He remembered that this was the woman who had tried to kill herself.

"He takes away my allowance."

They were talking around the problem, talking around what had just happened, or hadn't happened, between them.

"I don't get it," he said, frustration getting the best of him. He wanted solid answers. "Why did you come here? To spite him?" Then he had another thought, a thought that fit more with his original opinion of Sara Ivy. "Or was it to get yourself dirty, only to find you couldn't go through with it?"

She looked away, some of her newly regained composure slipping. "I . . . I, ah . . ." She swallowed. She pressed her lips together. "I was willing to make a trade," she said so softly he hardly heard her. "At least I thought I was." She shrugged her shoulders and let out a nervous little laugh. "Sex just doesn't seem to be a good means of barter for me." She clasped her hands together. "Perhaps if you'd wanted something else, anything else, it might have worked."

"What are you talking about?"

"Sex. That was your ultimatum, wasn't it?"

The room seemed to slant.

What had happened to him? How had he gotten so heartless?

There had been a time when he'd been more naive than Harley. There had been a time when he'd been a nice guy, too. And he'd been hurt. And he'd decided to get tough or be eaten alive. But this . . . Oh, God.

"I have to go."

Her words came to him through a thick haze.

"W-wait." Shaking, he grabbed a sweatshirt, then managed to stuff his feet into a pair of sneakers. "I'll walk you."

They made their way down the stairs, then down the hallway.

Outside, the moon was completely obliterated by snowflakes drifting earthward. They were huge—like tissue-paper cutouts, floating on the still air.

Sara's face was lifted to the night sky. "Snow." Her voice held the wonder of a child.

He watched as wet flakes kissed her cheeks, her hair, her eyelashes, melting against her skin. When she looked back at him, she was smiling. Not the self-mocking smile he'd seen earlier, but a soft, slow, real smile.

The wall he'd put up, the barrier he'd worked so hard and so diligently to build, crumbled.

And he knew, in that second, from that point on, that nothing would be the same.

He would never be able to look at the world with the same detachment, the same distance, the same lack of emotion.

They hadn't made love. Their bodies hadn't

joined, but *something* had happened. She had somehow, some way, touched his soul.

He, who had sworn never to love anyone again, watched her with a feeling of helplessness. He watched as snowflakes continued to fall on her face and hair and eyelashes.

A benediction.

He took one faltering step, then another.

Ever since the night on the beach, he'd known that he had to have her, possess her. But now everything had suddenly turned around.

Now he wanted more.

He stopped directly in front of her. Slowly, her face was drawn to his. Her smile faded. A question came into her eyes.

Slowly, carefully, he took her face in his hands, cupping her cold cheeks against his warm palms, watching as their breaths mingled. He lowered his head, watching as her eyes fluttered closed, as her face lifted to his.

His own eyes closed. And then there was just the softness of her lips.

Her hair slid over his wrist. Her hands came up around his neck.

He pulled her closer, bulky coat and all, his mouth moving over hers. Her lips parted, inviting his tongue. And when he slid it against hers, his heart pounded, his body throbbed.

A horn honked.

Reality.

A hand to her chin, he broke the kiss. Her eyelashes fluttered. She looked dazed, slightly disoriented.

"I'm sorry about what I said the night of Harley's party." His voice came out tight and strained and a little lost. "I sometimes say things I don't mean, just because . . . well, because I'm an ass." He brushed a finger across her bottom lip. "Come and see me anytime. We can play Monopoly. Or watch TV. Do you like to look at stars? I have lawn chairs set up on the roof of Shoot the Moon."

Honk.

She blinked, glanced over her shoulder, then back. "I have to go."

He wanted to extract a promise from her. He wanted her to tell him that she'd be back, that he would see her again. He loosened his hold and she slipped away.

She ran to the cab.

He followed, closing the door for her once she was inside. As the cab pulled away, he could see her watching him through the glass.

She lifted her hand in farewell.

Pathos. A word Harley had dug out of him, its meaning just now truly hitting home.

He lifted his own hand, the slow, lingering gesture mirroring hers.

How could one simple movement hurt so much? How could it be so bittersweet?